BEFORE
THE FUTURE

Ronald R. Crosthwaite

I0667735

AMENDED 10/20/2025

*This was originally published in 2017 when
I was 75 years of age.
Additions and adjustments have been made
for publication in 2025 at my age of 85*

PICFAIR
Publishing

Self Published under the name Picfair Publishing

Crosthwaite, Ronald R.
Before the Future

An autobiographical memoir including supporting photographs based on non-fictional events.
ISBN 978-0-9898447-2-7

Edited by Sharon Gorrell
Cover and design by
Ronald R. Crosthwaite

ACKNOWLEGDMENTS

I am grateful to my editor, Sharon Gorrell, for her guidance and accurate assessment of my story. I owe gratitude to all who have been a part of my life making this account of my journey possible. Without you there would have been nothing Before the Future.

*Dedicated to my children, grandchildren
and all who will follow*

INTRODUCTION

I was born November 29, 1940 at the Soto Street Hospital, which is no longer standing. The site is now a parking lot adjacent to the 1927 built Sears Building in the Boyle Heights District of Los Angeles, California. With the Sears Building's glowing green neon sign, the site is prominently viewed from many parts of the city. Several of the city's buildings and sites have vanished within my life-time. The ones that remain are familiar landmarks, such as the City Hall, Union Station, Clifton's Cafeteria and the Avila Adobe at Olvera Street. These landmarks and many more, of Los Angeles and its history, are mentioned in my stories. In my earlier days, San Diego landmarks are featured, such as the Presidio Park Museum and the Loma theater, as well as my grammar school, St. Charles Borromeo catholic school.

These are accounts of my memories through the times of my life from the age of four. Before that time, my life was pretty much childhood as usual. As I grew from that day forward, my life, like us all, took many twists and turns. Some are in the form of influences from my changing environment and others were pure survival. I, for the most part, grew up with a very weak male role model. My parents divorced when I was four, and until I was twelve, I was cared for by my aunt and uncle. My uncle, who loved me very much, wasn't a strong father influence. Through my early teens, back living with my mother, I had to re-invent myself by instilling self-confidence. I discovered humor through my mother's father, Ta Ta Al, and that became a way, of getting attention. Humor became measures of success, gaining confidence along the way and was one way I stumbled through those early years.

I've used humor ever since to obtain both approval and acceptance. It sometimes gets me into trouble, though, because too many times I speak without thinking hoping for a reaction. More than once, I've wished the words that spewed from my mouth could be taken back. To quote Cher, "If I could turn back time." But alas, the damage has been done. I'm reminded of my grandfather, who always seemed to speak with humorous intentions. I'm not sure I can stop. It's become a part of who I am. I do try to see the funny side of life and, for that reason, it has brought me that attention I so much seek. Attention is how I interpret acceptance and acceptance, seems to be the key to my need.

I find that many of my male friendships have centered around humor, starting with my first friend, Bill. I'm a big fan of comedians and comedy in general. It's interesting that my son Matthew has developed quite a good sense of humor. I love that about him. My cousin David also is quite the comedian. David and I produced a video in which he wrote the entire script. It include pun after pun starting with the news caster, Tom Brocow. It was all about a giant prehistoric cow called cowesoris rex that invaded the city. He acted in it while I filmed. We submitted it to 'America's Funniest Videos' but got no response. They don't know funny! When we three get together, usually on holidays, the corn flies. I'm always reminded of my corny grandfather. Good times. Good memories. Good feelings all-around.

Before the Future
INTO THE STORMY NIGHT
A new beginning

Plowing through the flooded streets in the winter of 1944, a late model sedan pulled up to the curb. Two occupants of the car made their way to a small Spanish colonial front door and knocked. No answer. They pounded on the door and waited. When the door finally opened, an old man appeared. There I was...beyond him in the kitchen. With no words spoken, they rushed past the startled man, knocking him onto the sofa. I was scooped up and before the old man could get up, we vanished into the shadowy darkness. The old man in hot pursuit tried to chase us, but his '29 Model A pickup was no match for the later model car. The plan to rescue me was a complete success as we escaped into the stormy night.

I was four years old and have no memory of where I was when my mother desperately searched for and found me. My aunt shed

Los Angeles Union Station

some light on this, and to her dying day, still hated my father. This so-called kidnapping is one of the reasons.

This melodrama was presented to me years later when I asked, "Where did I come from?" My mother and father divorced and, during one of my visits to my father, he chose not to return me to my mother. For over two weeks he would call my mother and put me on the phone and then hang up, torturing her to tears. My mother finally realized where I was and formed a plan. She and her sister, my Aunt Dee Dee, along with their cousin Lilly and her husband Walter, would go out that stormy night to rescue me. The old man in the doorway, who I was never to see again, was my grandfather on my father's side.

It was my mother herself who burst in, picked me up, and ran out the door. Losing my grandfather in the storm, they headed straight for the Union train station. My mother and aunt took me on my first train ride on the old locomotive to San Diego. That would be the first of many train rides back and forth from San Diego to Los Angeles. Forty years would pass before I was to see my father again.

After being relocated to live with my aunt and uncle in San Diego, those train rides back to Los Angeles I was to spend the summers with my aunt Jo and her family. Unknowingly, my father's brother Robert, who was in constant contact with my mother, kept

My father, me and my grandfather

my father informed of my whereabouts. When I was dropped off at the Union station my father stayed out of sight as he watched out for my safety until Aunt Jo was there to meet me.

Grandmother Osuna

Not much is known about my Grandmother Osuna. She died very young. Her husband, by grandfather, Ramon, never remarried. She had three sons, my father, Raymond, and his two brothers, Robert and Ralph.

I was to live with my aunt and uncle until my mother could get on her feet and

Hanging with Daddy

take me back. I remained with my new family for eight years before my mother came for me. It might have seemed that she was abandoning me; rather, she believed it to be a safe haven for me. My mother visited me quite often, but she didn't live with us. My aunt and uncle were responsible for raising me in those early years. They had children of their own, some, four and seven years later. Even though I was an only child, I didn't know what it meant to be an only child because I had two cousins as siblings with whom I grew up. I was given my aunt's married name of Hoagland, and my middle name was to become my first name, possibly to conceal my identity from my father. I went by the name of Ronald Hoagland until my mother re-married and came to claim her only child to start a new life.

I had everything a kid could want; two cousins who were like brother and sister, my mother, my Aunt Dee Dee, who was like a second mother, and my uncle Russ, who I was to refer as "Daddy." I'm sure he tried to be a father figure as best he could. His favorite pastime was fishing, so we did a lot of fishing… in a rubber raft, off the pier, on the lake, at the levy, wherever there was water and the slight possibility there was a fish to be caught, we were there. "Come

Uncle Russ (Daddy)

on, Ronnie. We're going fishing." Daddy would say, and off we went. My aunt would always pack a lunch for us fishermen and two empty jars. "What's the jar for? I asked. "When you're out there in the middle of the lake and you gotta go, you go into the jar." This was a new experience for me, "Peeing into a jar?" I thought.

At the time the family car was an old pre-war Ford sedan. I remember it seemed like every car on the road was black but ours was a light blue. "How come all the other cars are black and ours is blue? I asked. "We got this car used and it had been in an accident so we had it fixed and your aunt chose to have it painted her favorite color. So, see, that makes us special." Daddy said. I had never been special before, so I smiled contentedly. We got to the lake and launched the small aluminum boat Daddy had strapped to the roof of the Ford. I'd never been out on a lake and didn't even know how to swim. This was a little scary for me at age six. Daddy showed me how to take a slimy worm and poke a fishhook =through it while the thing wiggled in my hand, still alive. We eventually graduated to small bait fish that also wiggled. On my first try, the little sucker slipped out of my hands and into the lake. My uncle was a patient man and would tell me to give it another try. Eventually, I got the hang of it and, there we were, two fishermen, or rather a fisherman and a fisher-boy out there in the middle of the lake dropping lines, eating our bagged lunch, and peeing into a jar. As a boy of six, my thoughts weren't too profound, but I knew that this would be a special time spent with my uncle, who I called Daddy.

One time we drove the family car, a brand new shiny 1949 Ford, to Torrey Pines and did overnighter fishing off the shore in the

5

Me, Ronnie Hoagland, living at the *projects* 1947

breakers. We pulled the car out onto the sand and camped right there on the beach. The next morning we woke to find the surf lapping at our feet. The tide had come in overnight and swallowed up the car. Daddy was in big trouble then.

My uncle was a simple man, born and raised in Lincoln, Nebraska, with good morals and a kind and gentle heart. But all he really liked was fishing. I never learned how to play baseball, or any other sport for that matter. It just didn't interest him. Not until I had children of my own did I take an interest in sports. I learned, the hard way, how unpopular one can be if you can't join in the baseball game after school. I didn't carry on the tradition of fishing, but through it all, I value what my uncle taught me and, whatever goodness I might have, Daddy certainly contributed his share. Before he died, he asked that his ashes be spread out to sea. He said..."If I can't catch them, I'm going in after them."

My Aunt Dee Dee was the rock in our family. She looked after everyone, including my mother. We relied on her to always be there, and she was. She saw to it that we had a variety of foods on the table.

I remember before Chinese food was fashionable, we had it on our table. From peanut butter and jelly sandwiches to pot roast, she kept us well fed. Did I mention she didn't like fish? When my uncle got lucky and brought home the catch of the day, he was the one who would do the cooking. Ironically, it was Aunt Dee Dee who gave us our daily dose of Cod Liver Oil and looked after our bumps and scrapes. The only time I remember my uncle taking charge was when I crossed the street after having been told not to.

Aunt Dee Dee

The sting of his belt was all it took. I learned quickly.

We lived in housing called *"The Projects,"* provided by the federal government. My aunt and uncle met while working for Consolidated Aircraft, a government factory contracted to build warplanes for WWII. My mother worked there for a time before she followed her dream to be a hair stylist. She went to a school in downtown San Diego until she landed her first job in a small town north of the city called Oceanside, where, I believe, she met Ross (Cheno) Crosthwaite, later to become her second husband.

Uncle Russ and Aunt

It was 1946, and I was to take my second train ride, but this time I was all by myself. Waiting for the train at the dock was an experience in itself. I had to go to the front of the train to see the big black

Cousins Jody and Donna Dee and Me

engine bellow steam from its belly and feel the power of that enormous locomotive that was going to take me away down the tracks. Every summer for five years, I was put on the train bound for Los Angeles with a note pinned to my jacket. It had my name and who was to pick me up at the train station.

These trips became my introduction to a real farm. I would spend the summer with my Aunt Jo, my mother's half sister, her husband Uncle Nick and my three cousins Kathy, Jody, and Marky. The farm was located in Montebello, which at the time was a distant rural suburb of Los Angeles.

The strongest memories I have were of waking up early in the morning to the crowing of a rooster and the smell of fresh brewed coffee. I didn't drink coffee as a child, but to this day the smell of fresh brewed coffee takes me back to simpler times and fond memories. I remember the first time I tasted milk still warm from the cow. We would have a big breakfast with fresh eggs and pancakes and then, after a few chores, it was playtime.

My cousins and I would climb to the top of a huge haystack that was just outside the barn. Getting lost in a haystack and then being found if you made the slightest movement were one of the many games we played. There were chickens, ducks, geese, pigs, horses, cows and a bull. There was even a fishpond with the biggest gold fish I'd ever seen. Oh, and there was a dog and a few cats, too. There were acres and acres of corn and squash with irrigation ditches filled with water. Another tempting pastime was hiding among the tall stalks of corn and splashing in the muddy ditches. My aunt tolerated a lot but bringing the outside in was not one of them. Her home was immaculate and she wanted to keep it that way. I had my share of scoldings during those summers, but I was just a kid running free in the field and the mud. Once, I came face to face with the bull and was chased, barely escaping to the safety of the cornfields.

I remember looking out over the vast rows of planted zucchini, counting the cars on the freight trains that stretched across the horizon. The entire train of over a hundred cars could be seen as it slowly made its way past our playground. Into the distance, you could hear the haunting whistle that has all but disappeared, like the mighty black steam engines that used to roam this country.

Steam powered Locomotive

The *"projects"* is where I met my first honest to goodness best friend, Billy. I was five years old and he was six. That was in 1945

Billy, Ronnie, David, June (Billy's mother), Donna, Ricky and Natha
waiting for the bus to take us to Camp Cuyamaca

just after WWII. All I remember of the war was when we drove by
Consolidated Aircraft, where my family worked. We had to pass
under a huge net of camouflage that covered the entire road plus the
buildings. On occasion, there would be a practice dogfight between a
couple of fighter planes right over our home. Other than that, Billy,
me and everyone else our age were completely oblivious to this
historical event. Our job was to play. Billy had three brothers Ray,
David, Tony and one sister, Natha Anne. Because of us, our parents
became friends. We did everything together. Billy and I started the
first puppet show in the neighborhood. In fact it was the only puppet
show in the neighborhood. We played Cowboys and Indians, built
forts, and played hide and go seek yelling out "ali ali oxen free free
free" when all was safe to come from our hiding place.

We were bussed off to summer camp for a couple of weeks, each
year, where we learned to be on our own. Sleeping in cabins each
with our own bunk bed and eating in a mess hall was like being in the
army, although I didn't realize it at the time. Apple butter was always

Presidio Park Museum, San Diego

on the table to encourage us to eat our daily meals. A dab of this sweet, tangy goo became our way of downing food that was unfamiliar to us. To this day, eating apple butter reminds me of those innocent times. Our daily routine varied from going on a hike, crossing over a rope bridge, trying not to fall into the swimming hole below, to learning about nature and about the native people who lived in this region long before it was settled by the white man. At night, the counselors would tell us stories of Native Americans as we sat around a huge campfire. In the distance, we could hear drums echoing into the night sky as we sat mesmerized by the counselors' stories.

I remember when I got my first bike, a red and white J.C. Higgins with a battery-powered horn. Billy and I used to venture down to the creek that led to the sea, now Mission Valley. There, we would catch polliwogs and bring them home as our prize of the day. I don't remember any of those poor creatures turning into frogs. We eventually made it all the way to Presidio Park, where we explored the Presidio itself. In a way, it became our extended playground. I didn't know at the time that my great, grandfather six times removed, was stationed here and helped establish the first site of the Mission San Diego Acala at this present day location of the Presidio in 1769.

My ancestors took part in many important leadership roles to help settle early California. This included the first mayor of San Diego on my father's side and on my mother's side, the last Spanish governor of California. A novel including the full story of my ancestors' in California history is currently in the works.

Coming home from our adventures at the Presidio, Billy and I would join the rest of our neighborhood friends in anticipation of the TV show "Time for Beanie." A little curly haired blond girl named Geneva, who was always wetting her pants, had the first television set in the neighborhood. Without fail, we would all gather around her enormous 12" TV at 4:30 sharp to watch the show. Together we would cheer on Beanie, Captain Huff n' Puff, and Cecil the Seasick Sea Serpent, and boo Dishonest John the bad guy. Gathered around the tiny-screened television were John Pile and his two sisters, Gloria and big sister Carol, who knew too much for someone her age regarding the birds and the bees. They lived across the street and had a Collie named Rex.

To this day, when I see a Collie, I automatically think of Rex. There were the two sisters who lived downstairs from my cousins and me, Debbie and Lana. Lana was a very beautiful girl and all the boys, including me, had a crush on her. Of course, Billy and his brothers and sister, my two cousins Donna and Ricky, along with all the other kids, and I would sit in front of that magical new invention booing the villains and cheering the good guys. Little did we know this device was to take over the world, at least until the computer came along. Billy and I simply couldn't compete with *"Time for Beanie."* There went our puppet show.

Black and White
Television 12" screen

Loma Theater, Rosecrans Blvd., S.D.

On weekends, our parents would take us to the Loma Theater and drop us off for what seemed like an all day affair. *Superman, The Three Stooges, Laurel and Hardy, The Little Rascals, Flash Gordon* and *Tarzan* filled the screen and our imaginations. Each week's serial would show a continuing adventure from the previous week that would leave us hanging, wondering what was going to happen next...there we would be, the following week. Sure enough, the hero was saved, then it would start all over again. The theater is still there but it's now a bookstore. Luckily, the old theater theme was restored and looks just like it did in the old days, except for a few books. Those were very good times. Even after Billy and his family moved away into a real house in Imperial Beach, our families remained close. One Christmas, Billy and I both got our first Lionel electric trains. We linked all the tracks together and ran the trains all through the house.

During that time, my two cousins, Donna Dee and Ricky, and I went to St. Charles Borrameao, a Parochial school not far from the Loma Theater. My years there were pretty trying, to say the least. I had been taken out of public school because my grades weren't up to par. Catholic school was even harder. It was thought I would do better with a stricter environment...it didn't work. I did very poorly in academics but excelled in other activities such as music and art. I was in the school choir and learned some beautiful songs. I remember one song I was asked to stand up and sing in music class, "*Santa Lucia*." I've forgotten the words but I haven't forgotten the faces of the girls in the class as I sang. Probably a missed opportunity to become a rock star or something.

Ronnie, Donna and Ricky
at St. Charles Borrameao catholic school, San Diego

I joined the Jr. Safety Patrol while at St. Charles. This was an elite bunch of guys who got out of class early to don uniforms of red and white. We wore bright shiny badges topped off with a bright yellow garrison cap with a red trim. We looked sharp. We would march out to the street with our staffs of red and white and stop traffic for the students before and after school. I felt important for the first time. Once a month, we gathered by the hundreds from all over the city to parade down the streets of San Diego. Our destination was usually to file into a theater to watch a movie and receive a few awards. It was my first memory of belonging to a special group that warranted respect. On one occasion, while parading down the street, I remember a shiny white convertible Cadillac stopped at an intersection. The then famous actor Leo Carrillo was waving to us from his fancy automobile. I was to learn much later in life, that I am related to this icon of the silver screen.

Me, Jr. Safety Patrol

There was always a baseball game after school and all my classmates took part in the game. I usually just stood around hanging on the fence watching, wishing I could play, but I never learned. Being raised by my uncle where fishing was his only pastime, we never got around to playing ball.

I managed to get into trouble a few times. On one occasion, when the teacher had stepped out of the class for some unknown reason, I began to tap-dance. I only knew one step, but it only took one step for me be caught and put in the corner. I had to do that one step over and over until the bell rang. Bo Jangles I'm not. Maybe I was inspired by the story of when my mother danced for the famous movie star Loretta Young. To this day, I still enjoy dancing a great deal. I felt the sting of Mother Superior Mary Margaret's metal edged ruler, which drew blood, across the palm of my hand when I was caught drawing when I should have been reading. I made a career of drawing and I'm still not a good reader.

Mother Superior Mary Margaret portrayed here by Sally Strutters in "Nunsense"

Billy's family and mine picnicking in Presidio Park
My grandfather is in the back with his hat turned around;
way ahead of his time.

Before the Future

FROM GRASS TO ASPHALT

Downtown Los Angeles 1952

I really hated to leave all my family and friends, but when my mother re-married, she came to claim her son to try this family thing again. She married that fellow she'd met in Oceanside, Ross (Cheno) Crosthwaite. My name changed again. I was now known as Ronald Crosthwaite. I wasn't told my middle name at this time, but I don't think I even knew to ask. My middle name was actually my real first name, Raymond, which just happens to be the same as my fathers' first name, all though I wasn't a junior because my father's middle name was different than mine. I was born Raymond Ronald Osuna. Then, my last name was changed to my mother's second husband's name of Crosthwaite, which was changed from my uncle's last name, Hoagland. I honestly don't remember all this name changing being traumatic at the time, but I'll bet it's had its affect on me somewhere along the way. Anyway, it makes for good story telling.

We moved to Los Angeles and lived directly across the street from a huge hole in the ground on 5th and Hill Street, which was soon to be Pershing Square. Off to the upper right in the photo is the famed Biltmore Hotel.

Los Angeles City Hall

Next door to us was the Los Angeles P h i l h a r m o n i c headquarters, where, on several occasions, I w o u l d h e a r t h e m rehearsing. This could be where my love for classical music started at the tender age of twelve. We were right in the heart of the big city. I watched the first high-rise go up on 7th and Figueroa. The Hilton wasn't all that high, but it was the first building, after the City Hall, that began to change the sky line of Los Angeles after a moratorium on high rises because of the fear of earthquakes. Until then, in 1952, the City Hall was all of thirteen stories high. It was designed by John Parkinson, John C. Austen and Albert C. Martin, Sr., and was completed in 1928. Dedication ceremonies were held on April 26, 1928. It has 32 floors and, at 454 feet (138m) high, is the tallest *Base isolation* structure in the world. I worked for Albert C. Martin early in my career and designed the interior of the award winning Thousand Oaks Library, known as the Grant R. Brimhall Library.

We then moved into a more permanent residence on 7th and Union. It was a three-story apartment building with an elevator that didn't always work. We lived on the third floor. This was quite a

18

Pershing Square under construction. The Biltmore Hotel upper right corner

culture shock for me. From playing on grassy yards with old friends to the asphalt jungles of Los Angeles, where I knew no one. That was the summer of 1952. I spent a lot of time that summer going to the movies. The Orpheum Theater was the first of many elegant *Movie Palaces*, as they were called. I was on my own, taking streetcars for the first time in a city that was big and unfamiliar. I was forced to grow up fast and learn how to get around.

During those times, it was fairly safe for a youngster to roam the city, so I managed pretty well. The movies actually set the stage for the beginning of some of my personality traits. I began to imagine that the camera was on me at all times, and I had to be at my best. I became totally aware of myself. How I moved, how I looked, what I said. I was "on," as much as a twelve year old could be.

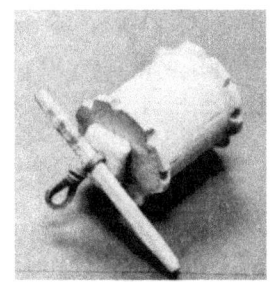

Toy tractor

The Orpheum Movie Palace

I met Elden the way kids met kids in the city, in the alley behind the apartment. We would go adventuring through the alleys and around the blocks doing a whole lot of nothing. We played some ball but not much. We learned from an old neighbor man, how to make simple toys like a tractor made from a wooden thread spool, a rubber band, a wooden matchstick, and some bar soap for lubrication. Another toy was a chatterbox from a tobacco tin. A rubber band was threaded through the tin with a piece of match stick in the middle, which was wound up carefully. Anyone who would slightly lift the lid caused it to make a chattering noise.

One Halloween we went trick-or-treating at the local bars and walked out with our pockets bulging with loose change. My city friend and I would go fishing in the lake at Westlake Park, now re-named McArthur Park. We would use a straight pin bent into a hook and some thread. We weren't very successful, much like my early

Westlake Park later to be known as Mac Arthur Park

fishing experiences. Little did I know but nine years later Westlake Park was to hold a very special place in my memories.

On our way to the park, we had to pass by a local strip joint that couldn't be missed for the pounding music that blared from its open door. There was a dark red velvet drape pulled across the opening that would bellow open and shut from the wind coming from the passing automobiles and streetcars traveling down 7th street. We would purposely slow our walk almost to a stand-still as we passed the red drapes trying desperately to catch a glimpse of flesh from the exotic dancer undulating on stage. We were constantly shooed away by the doorman who kept our adolescent eyes away from the mystery of sex.

When we made it to downtown we seemed to be drawn to the open-air newsstand trying to get a glimpse of the nudist magazines that were always on display. In those days all the interesting parts were blurred out, so we really didn't see anything. Our adolescent curiosity was alive and well as twelve year old boys.

Strip Club on 7th Street circa 1953

Our apartment had no bedroom so all three of us slept in close proximity. I slept on a makeshift bed that was a board spanning across the bench seats in the kitchen. My mother and her new husband, Cheno, slept on a pull-down bed in the living room called a Murphy bed.

One day, we were in Elden's apartment across the alley when we suddenly heard someone pounding and yelling at the front door. It was Elden's drunken father. The door was locked, and for good reason. I'm not sure who he was after and why he was so mad but we weren't going to wait around to find out. As he broke down the door I heard Elden's sister scream from the bedroom. When he entered the room, he grabbed an iron floor lamp, and bent it in half then started chasing us with it. It was Eldon's plan to jump out the front window to escape.

Eldon went first, showing me how to swing from the overhang of the second-floor ledge then drop to the concrete porch below. Apparently he had done this before. I followed him, but swung too far, and my fingers slipped. Down I went, landing flat on my back.

I've had the wind knocked out of me before but not like this. I immediately stood up trying to catch my breath, but just couldn't. I started running around gasping for air, but it just wouldn't come. I don't know how much time went by but there was my mother, trying to comfort me. By then, I could barely take air in, but couldn't expel any at all. I kept moving, walking around back and forth, pounding my fist on the lobby table. Nothing I tried

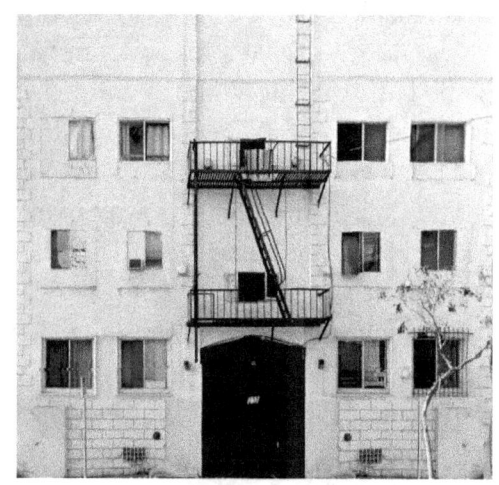

7th and Union Apartment

seemed to help. Just then I heard a siren. I could hear my heart pounding in my head like thunder.

When the ambulance arrived, I was put on a stretcher and whisked away to the emergency hospital with my mother at my side. Eventually, my breath came back, very slowly with small gasping sounds, in… then out. When they examined me they found no broken bones and released me. I was fine physically, but the ugly side of life was finding its way into my innocent world.

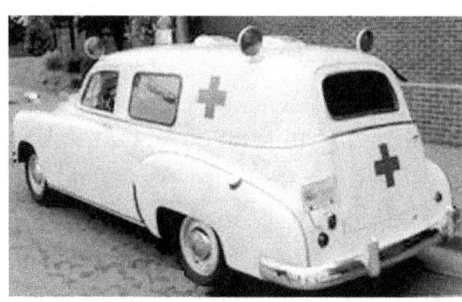

1952 Chevrolet ambulance

About this time, the story of the birds and the bees probably should have entered the picture. I learned, but from the wrong source. I'm sure my mother felt awkward about the subject, having not been there as I grew up. My stepfather, an ex-prize fighter, didn't care enough to play the father role. There wasn't much father-son relationship between us. When I brought out my electric train to play, he would say, "That's for children. Why don't you go outside and play some ball. Playing with toy trains is for sissies." Because of my lack of interest in sports, he would tease me relentlessly.

When the summer was over, it was off to Junior High. My mother took me to register. The man taking my information actually flirted with my mother, saying, "You must be the boy's sister. You look much too young to be his mother." My mother looked young for her age, and she had a flirtatious way about her, so as an opportunity would arise, she took full advantage of it. This always made me feel

uncomfortable. One story I've heard was when my mother was walking down the street, a man actually bumped into a lamp pole while watching her.

I was on my own again taking the 7th Street streetcar to the end of the line which deposited me right across the street from Virgil Junior High School. My grades improved my first year in Jr. High because of the much more advanced curriculum I'd experienced in catholic school. I now had my first girlfriend. I

Carrie, my mother at 32

used to walk her to class, walk her home and call her every night but I don't remember ever kissing her. We held hands.

A few memories stand out from living in such close quarters in an apartment with other tenants. We lived on the third floor, and the elevator didn't always work, so up and down the musty old carpeted stairs I climbed. Across the hall from us lived an Asian woman who taught me how to pick up the last remaining kernels of rice by pressing the fork onto the rice and capturing them between the prongs. The smell of meals being cooked, wafted throughout the halls

24

while young children scampered back and forth in the narrow playground outside of their apartments. From the third floor window, I would sail paper airplanes out across the open air. The memories aren't great ones, but they're stuck there in my twelve-year-old mind. Having a lot of time on my own, I began to develop a way of coping with my alone time. As I mentioned before, I imagined I was an actor in the movies and pretended a camera was on me at all times. I would move with poise and confidence as though my actions were being filmed.

At the end of my first year of junior high, I became aware of friction in my little family. The ex-prize fighter started coming home drunk. Sometimes he would bring a friend, and they would box and fight right there in the living room. Two big men rolling around in a small apartment made a lot of noise, and the furniture usually went flying. It was totally unfamiliar to me, and I didn't like it. One night the big boxer came home stinking drunk and pushed my mother down then grabbed me and started choking me with a belt. My mother screamed as a trickle of blood came from where the belt was pinching me. I guess the scream scared him because he ran out of the apartment. While he was gone, we gathered all our belongings and called my mothers' father, TaTa Al, to come rescue us.

ONE TWO THREE HE'S BACK

My Grandfather TaTa Al. on the right WWI

Everyone knew my grandfather as TaTa Al. I remember an old man, who didn't seem old at all. He was full of life, having something funny to say at every turn. I'm sure my exposure to him, gave birth to my sense of humor. I once asked him..."What do the initials M.G. on the British car mean?" He said, "My Gosh." He called my cousin Donna Dee, Donna Q and cousin Ricky, Rickshaw. It was my first taste of real corn. When he ended a sentence, he would let out a kind of grunt, like, "My Gosh-ugh." I wish I could remember more but I know it's in there in my genes, or something, because out of nowhere, I remind myself of him.

Pacific Electric line (Red Car) from Los Angeles, taken in 1909. This is the type of streetcar that struck my grandfather's mother takina her life.

TaTa Al was one of six children. At age eleven, his mother's life had been taken after being struck by a Red Car (the modern day rail system of the time, pictured) when he was still a boy. His father remarried a woman who had two children of her own. Apparently eight children were too much for his new bride to handle. My grandfather, along with his brother Lawrence, age eight, ended up in the Los Angeles County Orphanage Home in South Pasadena, the same city where I later was to purchase my first home.

When my grandfather left the orphanage he, joined the U.S. Army and fought in France during WWI, and earned the Purple Heart fighting the Germans. He was a sharpshooter in the Aragon 49th Division. Their slogan read 'Let Her Buck.' I have his walking stick with the slogan, along with the Division name, carved into it. When I joined the U.S. Army reserves at age 23, one of my summer camp tours was at Fort Lewis in Tacoma, Washington. This same fort is where my grandfather was trained as a young soldier a couple of generations before.

The Maryvale Orphans Home

TaTa Al married three times, and all three wives had virtually the same name. Some time after the army he married his first wife, Carmel. Until she gave birth to their son, it was unknown that she was a mulatto. The child's coloring was very dark, which proved to be an embarrassment to the family. Even though it was said that my grandfather loved his wife very much, family pressures caused an inevitable divorce. All that is known of the son is that he became a prominent Los Angeles attorney and went by the name of Argüello.

My grandfather's second wife was also named Carmel. She later was to be called Carrie, the name given to her by her employer when she became their nanny. When they met, Carrie was a widow with one daughter, Josephine, who was later to become my Aunt Jo. One year after their marriage Carrie gave birth to "the twins", my Mother and Aunt Dee Dee. My aunt got the nickname Dee Dee, when my mother was asked…"Who did it?" My mother as an infant would always point to her sister and say, "dee dee" trying to say, "She did it." The name stuck. My mother's nickname, Tootsie, was to come much later while in her teens. My grandmother, Carmel,

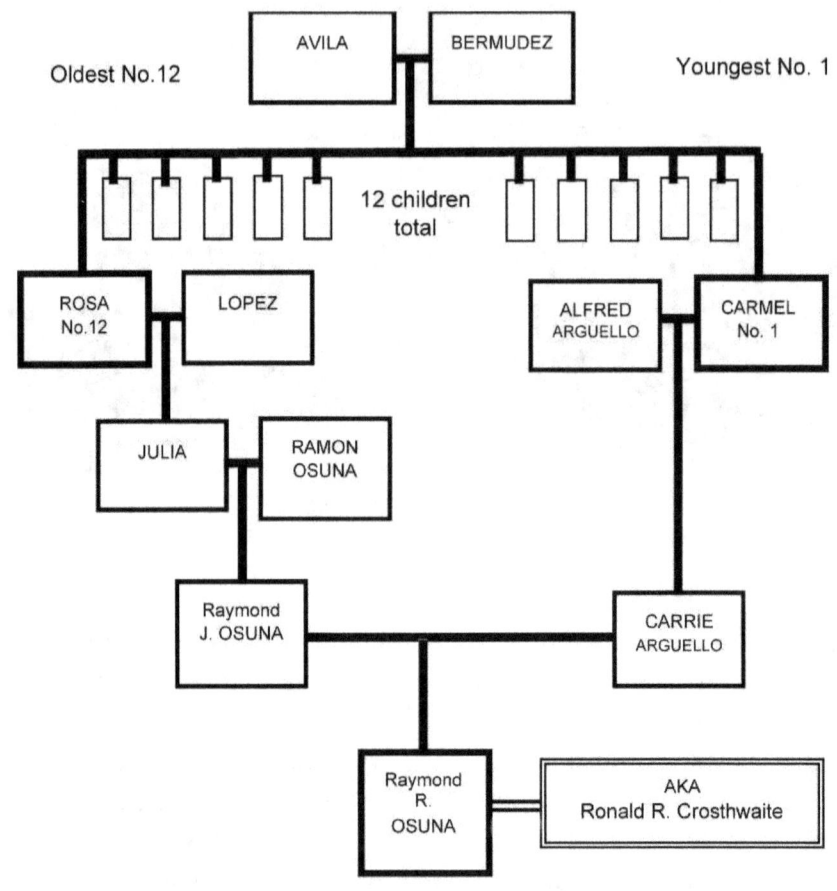

My Father and I have the same great grand parents

coincidentally was in an orphanage at the same time as her future husband, my grandfather, Ta Ta Al.

This is where the story gets a little convoluted. (See chart) Carmel, my grandmother, was the youngest of twelve brothers and sisters. Her oldest sister, now a mother herself, was given the task of raising my grandmother. I guess it proved too much for their aging parents to care for her properly. Eventually it proved too much for even Rosa, my grandmothers' sister. Carmel entered The Maryvale Orphans Home at the same age as her future second husband, Alfred,

Ta Ta Al and Carmel
my mother's parents

at age eleven. My father was the grandson of Rosa, which made my grandmother and grandfather second cousins. The irony here is that my father and I have the same great grandparents.

After about one year, the Scott family of Pasadena took my grandmother from the orphanage. They gave her the name of Carrie, which was to stay with her until her death. She was only twelve years old and was to become the nanny to the Scott's two children until she left to marry. She learned all there was to know about being a caregiver to a prominent family living in an up-scale neighborhood on Orange Grove Blvd. in Pasadena, California. It was this new exposure that gave her the training for being the refined lady she became.

She met Pete Montana and married. They had one daughter, Josephine, known to the family as Aunt Jo. Montana came to an untimely death on the job after only eight years of marriage. About two years later Carrie met and married my grandfather, TaTa Al. My Grandfather once again had the family he so much longed for. Within a year they had twins Carrie and Cecilia. My mother, Carrie, was given the same name as her mother's nickname. Because my grandmother had the knowledge of caring for a home in the best possible way, because of the conditions under which she lived in her early years, she insisted on giving her family all the benefits and comforts she had acquired as a nanny in a wealthy home. She had time to teach Josephine most of what she had learned, but by the time the twins came along she felt it was time to pour on the steam and do what she was trained to do all those years. She didn't let anyone lift a

Alfred (Ta Ta Al) and Carmel at Venice Beach 1919 (center left)

finger. The twins, especially, never really had to learn the domestic chores as their mother had labored over at such a young age.

When anyone came to visit, she always welcomed him or her with open arms, gracious hospitality, and good food. She was known for being kind to the homeless and would pass out food and give them a kind word. She furnished her home with the finest furniture and the most tasteful porcelains. They lived in a house left to Carrie by her former husband, Montana. Eventually, they built a larger home on the back lot of 721 Bailey Street in Boyle Heights. The house no longer exists, and where it stood is now a parking lot adjacent to the Golden State Freeway. Alfred always provided his family with the resources to maintain their lifestyle. Even during the Great Depression, he took any kind of work he could find in order to keep his family carefree and happy. The family never knew poverty. Among his jobs were

iceman and mail carrier. After a few years of hard work, he became a post office superintendent.

Their home had the best of everything, from furniture to dinnerware. Carrie was the perfect hostess, and Alfred was the ideal breadwinner. Things couldn't have been better until Carrie became very ill after a gall bladder operation and was suddenly taken from her family, to their complete devastation. It was said her doctor, at the time, had been on the golf course. No cell phones in those days.

My grandfather was utterly lost without her. She'd been taken from him after what he thought was another chance for happiness. He started to drink to drown his sorrows, but it took its toll. He neglected his daughters and the house. He began selling all of the fine furniture and dinnerware in order to support his drinking. Even the twins' possessions weren't spared. My mother and aunt were now without a mother at the tender age of fourteen, a time when the young sisters desperately needed guidance. It was as though time stood still for the twins. They really never got over the shock of having been

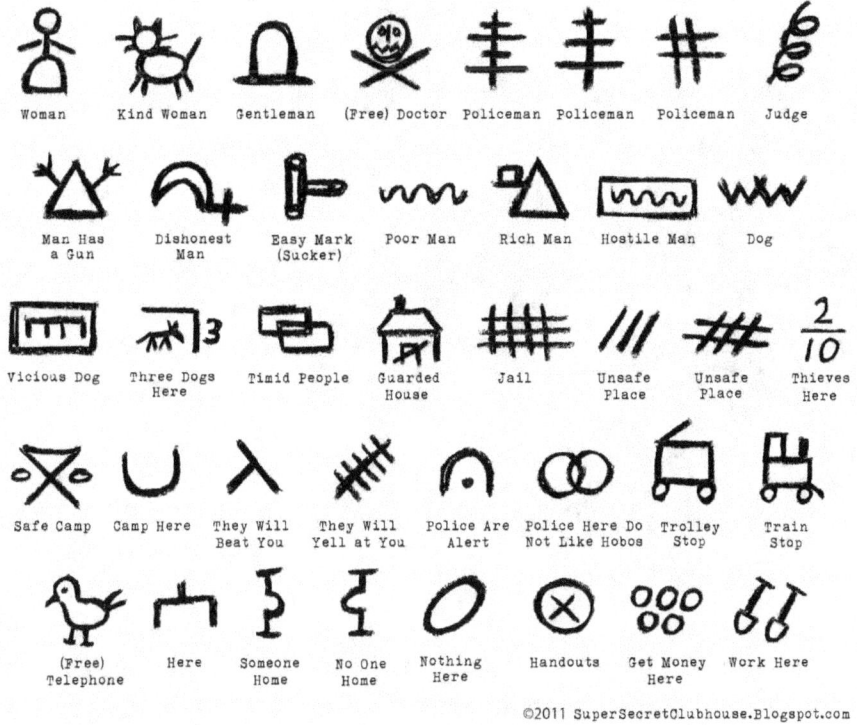

©2011 SuperSecretClubhouse.Blogspot.com

Hobo signs which helped to invite the homeless to my grandmother's door for a hand-out of food or water

abandoned. The mother who gave them everything they could ever want was gone, and their father was too lost in his own sorrow to offer any comfort. Their world ceased to exist. It just so happened my grandfather's drinking buddy was a family member, Raymond Osuna, my future father. As time went on and the twins got a little older, Raymond took an interest in Cecilia, my mother's sister. She refused his advances, so he moved on to my mother. They were married several months later, and I was the result of their union.

Grandmother Carmel Bermudez Argüello

The Antunez family, who were neighbors, stepped in and tried to fill the void caring for the twins as though they were their own. Over the years they had become like family. One of the Antunez's, Mary, had married Benny Argüello making our two families linked together by marriage.

Eventually, my grandfather sold the house. There was nothing left. By this time, Josephine had gotten married and hadn't suffered directly from the deterioration of the family. Several years passed before my grandfather was to meet his third wife. Her name was Carmelita. She brought with her a family of her own, but they were grown and married with children. Carmelita was the best thing that could have happened to my grandfather at that time. She

The Aline Barnsdall Hollyhock House is a building in the East Hollywood neighborhood of Los Angeles, California, originally designed by Frank Lloyd Wright as a residence for oil heiress Aline Barnsdall.

was a tough, no nonsense woman. Besides, she was bigger than him. He stopped drinking and actually came back to the living, sense of humor and all.

After my mother's bad experience with her second husband Cheno, we lived with my grandfather and his family for three months. TaTa Al was back with the City of Los Angeles as the park superintendent at Barnsdall Park. His designated living quarters was the guest home of the Hollyhock House, designed by Frank Lloyd Wright. It wasn't one of his famous houses but as I remember, it had many distinct characteristics of his more notable structures. Of course, I didn't know it then but when I got to Los Angeles City College and studied design I learned the history of where I had lived and felt very honored. The house has long since been demolished, but the memory of playtime in this great rambling home is still strong. My extended playground was the park itself, a seemingly endless back yard where my imagination ran wild with the freedom of my wandering. Some of my adventures through the park found me spying on young lovers lying on the grassy knolls overlooking the streets of Los Angeles. Barnsdall Park is an isolated hill in the neighborhood of Hollywood, bordering Sunset Blvd. on the south, Hollywood Blvd. on the north and Vermont Ave. to the east. It's now known as Barnsdall Art Park with galleries, workshops, and beautiful landscaped gardens.

Kaiser Hospital at the base of Barnsdall Park featured in the movie "Kiss me Deadly" staring Ralph Meeker and Cloris Leachman

I watched the construction of the Kaiser Foundation Hospital, at the base of the park. The building has changed a lot over the years but the address is the same. The hospital was featured in the 1955 movie "Kiss me Deadly." *One evening, private detective Mike Hammer (Ralph Meeker) picks up a strange woman, Christina (Cloris Leachman), who's standing on the highway wearing only a trench coat. They're stopped farther on by strangers who knock out Mike and murder Christina....*

Before the Future
OLD FRIENDS LOST

Frank, David, Lanny and Me

Mother and I moved from the Wright house to the back room of the beauty shop my mother and her cousin, Tina, bought. Once again, Aunt Dee Dee came to my mother's rescue. She put up my mother's share of the money by selling her dream property in the mountains. I don't know what made my mother choose the Lincoln Heights area to start her new business. I don't think she knew the kind of neighborhood it was. My new school and community were full of street gangs, all fighting one another and everyone else. A few of them wound up becoming friends of mine. They were always trying to get me to join their gang, The Little Avenues.

About this time, there were a few names being tagged on me, which I had to live down and fast. One was "chicken", the other was "mama's boy." Being called a chicken really didn't bother me. It made no sense to be called a chicken just because I didn't want to join a gang or fight for no apparent reason. Being called a mama's boy, however, didn't sit right, and I needed desperately to live that tag down. As I began to analyze my situation, I quickly knew what I had to do. Being an only child living with my mother seemed to be at the crux of my dilemma. My mother was trying her best to make up for all the years she hadn't been there for me. Unfortunately for her, the timing was bad. After all, I was a budding young man and needed my independence. I just sort of turned away and resented many things she tried to do for me. Don't get me wrong. A lot of what she did was for my own good. We ate out a lot, and she taught me about etiquette and manners, which I'm sure a boy in my situation might not have had a chance to learn. I became a very polite and well-mannered young gentleman. Everyone said so.

Alex

Five friends stand out during this time in my life. Alex Fonseca used to come over to my house and say, "Come on, we're gonna go beat up some guys." My standard answer was, "No thanks." When he came back from his little outing we would wrestle and roll around, and I always got the best of him, even though he was almost twice my size. Mind over a lot of matter. He had the walk and the look, but was really harmless. After he graduated from high school, he became my first roommate and was dating a young girl who worked for my mother in her beauty shop. Alex joined the U.S. Air Force, as an Air Policeman. When he left the Air Force he became a private investigator.

38

Frank

Frank Vulo, the Italian lover. Frank lived in the fanciest house on the block. We all thought he was rich. He was just Italian. His house was filled with every tchotchke known to man, statues, paintings, bottles filled with colored water, multi-layered rugs, and blue walls. His home was nothing like any of us regular guys' homes. Having the reputation of being a lover, we all wanted to have him tell us details of his conquests. We lived for his juicy stories. Whatever happened to Frank Vulo?

Lanny Holloway, the fat kid. I remember his daily trip to the local market coming back with a very large bag filled with potato chips and sodas. One day we were fooling around with knives and I accidentally cut him on the palm of his hand. All I can think of was that white blubbery stuff oozing from his wound. Lanny followed in his fathers' footsteps and became a city bus driver. I caught up with him many years later at a reunion of one of my friends. Her girlfriend had married Lanny, and there he was. We had some good laughs catching up on old times.

Lanny

My best friend then, David Alvarez, was both my mentor and my protector. David worked out and, lucky for me, was very intimidating. He was the one who helped me with that "mama's boy" thing. Years later I learned that he was my mothers' mailman. I looked him up and tried to renew our friendship but he was having some hard times and had started hitting the bottle. I'd had my share of bad memories already relating to booze, so I moved on.

David

We all attended Nightingale Junior High School, which happened to be right across the street from my mother's beauty shop on North Figueroa. I was in my second year coming from Virgil Junior High School on Vermont, where I started school after coming to Los Angeles. This school was populated with many gang members and one of the gangs, called Little Avenues, was very prominent. Good or bad, I was mistaken for their gang leader. Apparently I looked just like him. In order to blend in and not be harassed, I would wear the same type of clothes worn by the gang members of the day. Khaki pants with the cuffs ironed down to a half inch wide, a white tee shirt and, of course, a leather jacket. The shoes were black lace up with a pointed tip. They were spit-polished so shiny you could see your reflection in them. Last but not least, the hair was worn in what was called a "duck tail." Usually, our hair was slicked down with a gel-like substance like Vaseline or Brylcreem. I lost contact with those friends when I transferred to a high school out of my district.

After graduation from Nightingale Jr. High, Billy Palone and I jumped on a streetcar and headed to downtown. It was our big day and we were going to do whatever

Billy and me

40

came into our minds. First stop, Chinatown to buy some firecrackers. Next, we took in a couple of double features at the grand theaters along Broadway. We ate at the famous Clifton's Cafeteria and finally made it home close to 11pm. Our celebration was complete. I also lost contact with Billy.

My mother finally realized our home wasn't in the best neighborhood. She wanted me out of there. Thanks, Mom. We lived in the Lincoln High School district where there was an unsavory atmosphere of gang related population. Somehow, my mother was able to get me into Franklin High School in Highland Park, far away from my gang infested neighborhood.

Chinatown, Los Angeles

❖

Clifton's Brookdale Cafeteria
My mother and her twin sister Cecilia went there as children in 1935.
The famed cafeteria has since become a hot spot for dancing
and a social gathering for young Angelinos.

Before the Future
FAMILY TRADITIONS

| Angie Nina | Betty Anne | (front row) | Francine | Auntie Francis | Dee Dee |
| Aunt Lou | Uncle Irish | Joe Tombrello | Ronnie | Russ Donna Dee | Carrie |

My mother and I started to do a lot of family visiting once we got settled in our new home. We went back to her roots and back to the early traditions I had missed out on during my life in San Diego. The Antunez family still lived in the same house in the old Boyle Heights neighborhood. Their backyard parties were famous for bringing family and friends together from all over. Flank steak wrapped in a flower tortilla with homemade salsa, home cooked beans, and all kinds of desserts. That's what I remember best. All the men would gather around the fire pit and tell Uncle Irish how to cook. All you could hear was constant arguing about when to turn the meat over. It was tradition. There were never fewer than fifty people at these gatherings, and sometimes as many as two hundred plus. We kids would play in the huge back yard with toys that dated beyond my mothers' childhood. Of course, there was alcohol but no one ever got out of hand.

Traditionally everything from birthdays to wedding receptions played out in this backyard. I'm so glad I was able to experience those gatherings. The two families that so long ago had merged in holy matrimony were still carrying on the traditions of their early days.

Angie was one of nine brothers and sisters and the matriarch of the Antunez family. Her soul was as kind as a saint. She was a large, gentle old woman by the time I met her. (Remember, I was only fourteen years old and everyone seemed old to me.) She was probably no older than sixty-five or so. We all called her Angie Nina. Nina means aunt in Spanish. It all sort of ran together and sounded like...Anganina. She lived with her brother, Irish, and two sisters, Aunt Lou and Aunti Frances. I had always thought I was Irish because of that name. Only much later did I find out that I really am part Irish.

Aunt Lou's son, Johnny, at twenty-one, was killed in a boiler room explosion while serving in the U.S. Navy during WWII. We were all there at the house during a family gathering when the telegram arrived. To this day, I still have Johnny's Navy 'P' coat, given to me by Aunt Lou, even though I never knew him.

Aunti Francis was quite the high roller in her day and tough as nails. After her divorce she and daughter, Betty Anne, moved into the small guesthouse in the back of the main house. Betty Anne married Joe Tombrelo, a welcomed new member of the family and together went on to raise six children of their own, carrying on the tradition of the large family.

Uncle Irish never married. I don't think there was a woman alive who would have him. He was the most ornery, cantankerous, argumentative, old grouch I had the pleasure of knowing. He seemed to hate kids, always yelling at us from his big old chair, with a deep gravelly voice that scared the wits out of us. Poor old guy. He probably just felt helpless living with a bunch of women. Once you got to know him, or grew up a bit, he really wasn't so bad.

Uncle Irish

Anganina never married either, but you'd never know it. She must have picked up the fine art of cooking from her mother because everything she touched in that kitchen turned to gold. She was the best cook ever. I have never tasted homemade tamales like hers. Her albondigas soup was famous. Anganina's home was always open. She was ready to feed you as soon as you walked through the door.

The youngest brother, George, was an L.A.P.D. officer. I remember he and his buddy Robert, an old-time friend of the family, would come over while still in uniform. Two big men dressed in their dark blue uniforms coming through the door used to intimidate us kids, but these guys were family and once inside all was fine. They would talk shop, and we would all sit around and listen to them expounding on their day on the force. The stories always had a funny side, but some were serious and a little scary.

TaTa Als' father, my great grandfather, had also been on the force. As a matter of fact he was one of the first "keystone cops" in Los Angeles. His badge remains in the family to this day and reads Los Angeles Police Department Badge #17. He was with the police force for thirty years and retired as captain.

Some of the more colorful stories passed down were that Alejondro Alfredo Argüello, the cop, was somewhat of a practical joker. He would break up a bunch of guys gambling and pocket the

45

Aunt Lou,   Daddy,   Anganina,   Aunt Dee Dee,   Aunti Francis   and

money. When he was directing traffic, he would wave his arms and shake his behind in all kinds of gyrations giving the motorists a show to remember. Not cruel or shady, but a bit non-professional. All in all, he was known as quite the character. In those days I'm sure he got away with more than he should have but who am I to judge, after all he created some colorful history.

Another family my mother and I would visit was her cousin Lilly and family. I met my second cousins, Lorelei, Carol Anne and Dougy the youngest, until two more girls came along. Terry was the first of the two latecomers. We called her "Terrible Terry." She learned fast, always into trouble or just bugging us older kids. She had a devilish look in her eyes and an endless amount of energy that kept everyone guessing. (The picture of the cousins was taken before Judy came along. The youngest shown is Terry sitting on her oldest sister, Lorelei's lap.)

The Antunez home is still there in Boyle Heights and just missed
being torn down when The Golden State freeway went in.
The family and '49 Packard are long gone.

When Terry grew up, she fell in love with a man who met her
match. Gary can only be described as the one who tamed Terrible
Terry. Together, they make a considerable team. Ironically, Terry
turned out to be another "Mother Teresa" to the family, always there
in a crisis. Their son Justin was taken from us in an auto accident
much too soon. Their daughter Sibyl is a sweet, vivacious young lady.
She carries a little of that spark of life her mother had.

The second latecomer to the family was a beautiful little blond
girl with laughing eyes and a sort of sweet shyness about her. Judy
was the final second cousin to join the group. She and her husband,
Ken, have three children, two boys and a girl.

Dougy was always off with his friends and wasn't around
much. He served his country in the Army as a cook for twenty years.
After retiring, he went back to school to become a teacher to serve his

community in Texas where he met his bride. They, too, have three children and all still live in Texas.

Meeting these cousins for the first time as an adolescent and getting attention from two cute girls, even though they were my cousins, was quite a treat. I liked it. I'm sure I even had a kind of crush on Lorelei. She even enticed me to take my first drag on a cigarette when I was fourteen. I didn't need any more than that one time to convince me that this wasn't for me. When we got a lot older, we used to go dancing at the El Monte Legion Stadium. It was the place to be. All the famous rock and roll legends of the day were featured there. She went looking for guys, and I went looking for girls. It was a pretty good arrangement.

Years later, after she had married and divorced two times and was strapped with five kids, I introduced her to my old buddy George, and they dated for a while. Her oldest daughter, Susie, then 19, moved away to live with friends in Arizona and was in a fatal auto accident that took her from us all. It was tragic losing someone so young. Lorelei's other four children have all married and have kids of their own.

I had also introduced Carol Anne to two of my buddies, Alex and David, but she moved on and eventually met the right man. Jim has given her many years of comfort with a steady work ethic giving her and their three children security and the comfort of a worry free home.

Danny, the eldest, the only boy and a former Marine just like his dad, served in the Desert Storm Campaign. He now works with his father in the moving business and is the sales manager for residential moves. He also, along with his wife Kathy, has a small business producing an old family recipe of pickles called "Hoopers Pickles." Danny Hooper has a son, Nicholas, who is an exact clone of his father in every way and ironically is being raised by the same parents who raised his father, Carol Anne and Jim. It all has happened through an unusual turn of events that makes for an interesting arrangement but it seems to be working just fine. Danny is now married to Kathy who

Alejondro Alfredo Argüello Los Angeles Police 1909

has a son from a previous marriage and near the same age as Nicholas. Danny has coached both his sons on the same little league team. Both boys get along probably better than most brothers.

Carol and Jim's next child, Christina, is married to one of her brothers' Marine buddies and they have two children, Natalie and Renee. Both Christina and her husband, Rudy, work for Jim in the moving business. The third child is an energetic and creative young lady full of life and ready to take on the world and is married. Mary has her sights set on a career in marketing. They now have a set of twins.

Carol Anne is now the spokesperson for her immediate family. We are, and always have been, the closest of all the second cousins. We're the same age and have tried to be the level headed ones in our respective families. She and I will speak only three or four times a year, but boy, does the gossip build up. We fill each other in on all that has happened since we last spoke.

Dougy   Donna Dee   Diane,   Lorelei,,   Carol Ann Danny
                                  Terry   Ronnie
                                      Ricky   Kenny

One of my favorite family stories was about Danny Arguello, my contemporary. Danny was always getting his share of attention from our two cute girl cousins Lorelei and Carol Anne. He was blessed with a great sense of humor and kept us in stitches with his quick wit.

Although we lost touch as adults, Danny made his mark in the family legend because of a little vacation. He went to Guadalajara one summer and met the girl who stole his heart. Apparently, the father of Danny's new love wouldn't let her leave the country to marry. He said if Danny married his daughter and lived in Mexico, he would set him up in any business he desired. Danny only knew one business, pizza. He had managed a Shakeys Pizza Parlor in Downey, California, and threw pizzas in the air for a living.

Given the choice of leaving his heart in Mexico or having both a business of his own and the girl of his dreams, Danny had only one decision to make…what to call his new business. Papa Bambino's

Pizza became the only pizza parlor in Guadalajara. After the first year in business Shakeys Pizza offered to buy him out for one million dollars. Danny held fast and opened two more locations. He enjoyed the good life for many years. Danny and his bride raised four children, Daniel, Patrick, Billy and Debbie. They were all at their fathers funeral when Danny was suddenly taken from us after his fifty fourth birthday. Patrick now works for Jim in the moving business.

El Monte Legion Stadium circa 1957
The famous radio DJ Art Laboe is on the right.
Lorelei and I must be there somewhere in the crowd.

Before the Future
SURPRISE...SURPRISE

Cousin Ricky, Leona, Candy and cousin Donna Dee

My mother and I finally moved from the back of the beauty shop into a very small house located at the back of the home of Sam and Grace Magno. Grace was one of my mother's customers and offered this little tiny house they had built for a family member. We called it "The Match Box House."

The Magno's were a real, authentic Italian family from the old country. I followed some of their family traditions, mainly around the dinner table, and made them my own. Thursday night was always spaghetti night. That's when my mother and I were invited to enjoy a good old fashion Italian dinner. Sam was always at the head of the table and was served first. The standard drink served at each meal was Ginger Ale, which I had never had before. Needless to say the homemade sauce was sensational. Then came the salad. It was tradition that after all were served, Sam was presented the huge salad bowl to finish what was left. I adapted those simple traditions for my own and am grateful to Grace and Sam for the introduction.

My mother and I fit pretty well in our little home until some unexpected guests appeared. We would visit my grandfather and his family almost every weekend for barbecues and family visiting. At one of these gatherings, my mother met her third husband, Leo. He was the son of TaTa Als' third wife, Carmelita. He had three daughters and a son from a previous marriage. Before I knew it, though not married to my mom, Leo and his three daughters moved in with us in that small house. The son stayed with his mother. There we were, six people in a matchbox. There were two adjoining bedrooms, which were only separated by a curtain. My mother and Leo slept in the living room and the three girls and I shared the two bedrooms.

It was very strange, to say the least, for a fourteen-year-old boy to share his domain with three strange little girls. Gloria the oldest was eight, Leona was six and the youngest, Candy, was four. My mother did her best to create a comfortable home environment but it was still quite awkward. About this time I was starting high school and needed study space. I believe my studies suffered as a result of having very little privacy.

This arrangement varied from time to time, with one or more of the older girls going off to live in a Catholic boarding home. After I graduated from high school, we moved to Highland Park into a much larger home. I was surprised when my mother and Leo came back from a long weekend and broke the news to me that they had gotten married.

HERE COMES AUNT LILLY

Aunt Lilly claimed to have worked for Al Capone, gangster in the 20's

Why not fill the new, larger house to capacity? A new guest was now to arrive. Here comes Aunt Lilly. One of the family members responsible for caring for my mother when she had lost her mother was her Aunt Lilly, my grandfather TaTa Al's sister. Aunt Lilly had been missing for many years and was found by my mother's Cousin Lilly, who found Aunt Lilly and told my mother of her whereabouts. We were led to an address in South Central Los Angeles. Aunt Lilly had suffered a stroke several years previous and was now living in a small back house of a black family. She worked at a laundry with all blacks and was living in an all black neighborhood. After her stroke, she became black. The family in the front house looked after her like she was one of their own. She was there for many years and had assimilated into the sub-culture.

Crazy Aunt Lilly is what we called her. She wasn't crazy, just a little eccentric. Apparently in her day she was quite the swinger. She

55

claimed to have worked for the infamous Al Capone, the famous mobster during the 20's, bottling gin in her bathtub. It was told that she actually got married on roller skates. That was in her younger days. Now she was a character of a different type. She was our soul sister. She used to get calls all the time from her sisters in the 'hood. When I answered

A wedding on roller-stakes

the phone I'd hear...'Hello, Lilly there?'...in a very strong, high pitched black drawl. She would get on the phone, and you would swear she turned black before your eyes. They would shuck and jive and laaaugh...they seemed to be having the time of their lives.

Aunt Lilly brought with her an interesting way of speaking and a politeness that charmed us all. When asked if she wanted something from the dinner table she would reply, "If you please." When she was delighted with some tasty morsel, she would utter, "hm...hm...hm"... She would always want to help around the kitchen, but when we went to put the dishes away, we usually had to wash them again. She meant well. Aunt Lilly was a bit on the heavy side with skinny little legs that could barely hold her up. She would fall quite often, but had a quaint way of explaining her new position on the floor. I remember more than once coming home from college and finding her there on the floor with one leg propped up and an arm behind her head pretending to be cooling off in front of the fan. Her favorite chair was an old rocker. When it was time to get up, she would rock back and forth several times, gathering her momentum, then up she went. She wasn't always successful so we would give her a little boost. When my friend Mickey would come over, she would always look at him for help and while he was pulling her up she would give his hand a little squeeze. She thought he was cute. Whenever I was leaving the house to go out on the town, she would ask me if I had my stiletto.

Sometimes Aunt Lilly would sit on the front porch and watch the traffic and the people pass by. One day, when I came home, I found her with a visitor. An old gentleman caller was sharing her front porch, only he wasn't interested in the view. One day he had his hand on her knee. The next day I came home to find them in the back yard where he was sharing his bottle of wine. She was diabetic and wasn't supposed to be drinking. I asked him to please keep his wine away, and he did. The coup de grace was the day I came home and heard a noise coming from her bedroom. When I got closer to the door, there was no doubt to what was going on. The poor old gentleman died a week later...Aunt Lilly still knew how to swing.

Aunt Lilly

Before the Future
LASTING FRIENDSHIPS

Ron   Pat   George

In my last year in junior high, I had done okay, but high school frightened me. My grades proved it. I joined the R.O.T.C. my first year instead of gym class, but finally got tired of the uniform. By the second year I joined the ranks of the common boy and donned the gym uniform consisting of blue shorts and white T-shirt. This is where I met Pat Moran, my racing buddy. We were about equal in all those gym competitions. I guess that's what brought us together. Pat just saw life as one good time, and we made the most of it.

There wasn't much Pat took seriously except eating. He would come to my home and eat dinner with my mother and me, then immediately go and have a second meal at his girlfriend's home. He

Pat

would then go to his own home and eat another dinner! We went everywhere in his 1949 blue Ford. When we weren't cruising you'd find Pat under that car cussing up a storm. He had to. It was the only way he could fix that old Ford.

When I met Pat's parents, I could see right away that innocent goodness from his mother and that plow-through-at-all- costs attitude from his father. His mother reminded me of the kind of woman who had came across the prairie in a covered wagon. She was silent and steady as a rock, nurturing Pat and his two sisters, Rita and Virginia, with every fiber in her body.

Pat's father was a true Archie Bunker/Homer Simpson type with a twist. He, like his wife, was all good. Oh, he made comments about one thing or another but you could tell there was never any malice intended. He loved to talk to me and give his opinion but he always wanted to hear my opinion too. He made me feel important.

One of the most memorable moments I had with Mr. Moran was the time I was coming home from summer school on the bus. It was the first and only time I happened to catch the bus he was driving. His face lit up when he saw me board...It was show time! He drove that bus like a madman. A horn blew as he began to pick-up speed. He waved to the irate driver as though he knew him and kept accelerating. We were coming up on a stop with the 5 o'clock rush anxiously awaiting their ride home. The bus stop was on a curve in the road. The road dipped away from the turn, causing one to slow down considerably to negotiate the turn. We didn't slow down. We just kept plowing through the turn. Passengers were flying everywhere. The ones standing fell into people's laps, packages tumbled down the aisle and I couldn't stop laughing. The people at the bus stop were just a blur of frantically waving arms.

George

I met my church-visiting buddy, George Hardy, my first year of high school. I was standing in the cafeteria line and from behind me I heard..."Are you Catholic?" For some stylish, reason I was wearing a crucifix around my neck at the time and he assumed I was Catholic. Although I had gone to Catholic school I guess wearing that cross made me look Catholic. I had not attended church since coming to Los Angeles and my mother never enforced the church thing so I just drifted but when George saw that cross around my neck and asked if I were catholic, I just had to say yes. Maybe George didn't know too many Catholics and I was somewhat of a novelty. George was a very personable guy for someone his age. I'd never met anyone like him before. He seemed very grown up. Later, when I met his parents, I understood why. His father was an accountant and his mother was a legal secretary. She had a sort of New England accent, or at least she sounded very proper. It reminded me of some of the movie characters I'd grown to admire. George's parents, were serious people and avid readers. I'd never seen so many books in someone's home. They were very warm and delightful people. I was always welcomed with a smile and stimulating conversation.

Being brought up by such parents gave George a dimension one doesn't often see in a high school teenager, confidence. He had an unusual interest at the time we met. He shared that interest with me, which turned out to be visiting houses of faith. Each Sunday we'd visit a different church. We started with St Sofia's Greek Orthodox

Saint Sofia's Greek Orthodox Church

Church, then next, a black Southern Baptist service. He always had someplace to go and I was right there tagging along learning every step of the way. We were in the high school choir together which added another common bond to our friendship.

George is responsible for introducing me to coffee. Our job was to hang out at the local ice cream parlor, Fosselman's, and drink coffee and watch the endless parade of girls. Slowly, as my refills diluted my sugar-saturated coffee, I began to develop a taste for black coffee. On one

Dress up Day at Franklin High School

occasion when Pat Moran was with us, he challenged Bob Fosselman, the owner, to an eating duel. The object was for Pat to eat three banana splits in a row. If he finished all three they were all free. I don't think Mr. Fosselman knew who he was dealing with. Well guess who won? Pat remains skinny to this day…Maybe his secret is the length of time he spends in the john.

The Argonaut senior prom decoration

High school wasn't too eventful for me. I started with choosing to join the ROTC instead of gym class. One semester of that was enough. My grades were at a cool 'C' average. Academics were not my strong point. I was somewhat shy, especially with girls. I had a girl friend, which kind of kept me in check socially.

The only activity I excelled in was choir. I had a pretty decent voice and was able to move up within the choir to a select group of twenty called the 'clef dwellers' led by our choir director Don Gustafson. The school was putting on a western theme play, and the choir was selected to participate. I entered the audition to sing in a quartet performing "The Streets of Laredo." I won the part as the soloist, but was aced out by one of the quartet members who was actually taking singing lessons. The choir director thought it more prudent to choose the other fellow over me because it was assumed he would follow his path professionally. There went my chance to be a star. That same quartet sang for our graduation at Oxy Bowl at Occidental College where President Obama had attended. We were scheduled to sing "The Halls of Ivy", but when it came time for rehearsal, we surprised everyone with a little tune called, "Yakkity Yack." I could only live vicariously though my daughter when she performed as a soloist on stage at her high school. She was very

63

The Clef Dwellers directed by Don Gustafson

successful and went on to have the lead role in all three of the musicals she was in. Other than choir, the only other place I excelled was designing and directing the installation of my class senior prom. Because of our class name, the Argonauts, the theme was called "Under the Sea." I can't help but think of the similarity between the "Back to the Future" movie having their prom theme named "Enchantment under the Sea."

❖

Before the Future
DREAMS ARE FOR REAL

Doctored image from the movie *The Day the Earth Stood Still*

My old friend David Alvarez set me up with a girl with whom I went steady my first year of high school. Through it all, I was very loyal and having a good time to boot. We even ditched school one time and boldly took the streetcar to downtown L.A. so we could go to the movies and neck. I met her at the bus stop every morning before school and walked her home every day. Any chance we got we would do a little more exploring. Walk and neck; walk and neck; walk and neck.

On one occasion, when it just started getting dark, we decided to take a short cut. We walked along the railroad tracks behind the main street so we could do a little more exploring. As we stood there holding each other, gazing at the night sky, we both saw a shooting star. We started to look for more and suddenly saw something neither of us was prepared for. We saw, for an instant, what we thought to be another shooting star...but this one stopped, then zig zagged back and forth about two or three times, then shot off in another direction and disappeared into the night sky. Our jaws dropped as we slowly turned toward one another in disbelief. Our exploring led to something much more than we expected. The fact that we both saw this phenomenon at the same time convinced us that we were not alone in this universe. I had, on two other occasions, seen similar unexplained lights in the sky and shared them with my girlfriend. A year had passed, and the new semester was about to begin. The night before the new semester, I had a very unusual dream, which was to affect me for the next several years. The dream was about the visiting of aliens from another world.

Adrienne my high school girlfriend

The dream:

A UFO flew over the neighborhood and appeared to be landing. The news spread fast and it seemed everyone was rushing toward the local high school where it had come down. When I got there I noticed the saucer–like object was on the ground and hundreds of people were sitting on a cable that was stretched across the fifty-yard line. We all watched in silence, with a kind of nervous anxiety. All of sudden a door of the saucer started to open and a bright light burst out into the darkness. People began screaming and running in all directions scrambling for their lives. A girl who had been sitting on the cable in front of me stumbled to the ground. I helped her up, and we both

66

began to run. I never let go of her hand, even after we found a place to hide.

When I awoke that next morning my heart was pounding and all I could think of was that girl. She completely captivated me. I couldn't get her out of my mind. With all of the excitement of the new semester and the beginning of my new Spanish class, I had forgotten the dream, until...through the door, walked the girl in my dream.

I was shocked. I stood up with a jolt. My mouth fell open and my heart began to pound in my chest. As I slowly sat down, I couldn't take my eyes off her. When I got home that day I called my girlfriend and told her I couldn't see her any more...just like that. I gave her no explanation. I wasn't even thinking of her feelings. I completely ignored her and wouldn't even speak to her throughout the rest of high school. I was still very shy and really had no confidence in new encounters, especially one of this kind.

Kathy Strong
the girl in the dream

I walked in the shadows of this dream girl, never daring to talk to her. I had joined the choir that year and to my surprise she had also joined. I was a tenor. She was a tenor. She stood right next to me as we sang. Her brother, Mickey, was also in the choir and we were to become close friends although at the time I didn't know they were brother and sister. As time went by she and I became good friends. I was a frequent visitor to her home while visiting her brother. My mother even started cutting her mother's hair. I wound up getting a ride to school every morning with her brother and her. We were always together on our choir outings. Christmas caroling was especially an important memory for me. Though she was one of the most popular girls in the school, I was usually nearby in the shadows. Everyone claimed to be her best friend, but I was the only one who'd had the dream.

I never got the nerve to ask her out, although many years later she confessed that if I had, she might have said yes. Through most of high school, she seemed always to have a boyfriend, so there really wasn't much opportunity for me to be so bold as to make a move. The closest I got to her was taking her best friend to my senior prom. That summer after high school, we would spend a lot of time

My Senior Prom night with Marlys Miller
Franklin High School S'58

together while her fiancé was away in the Air Force. I even taught her to drive. We went on to the same junior college along with my old buddies Pat and George. Pat gave Kathy and me thrill rides to school in that same old blue '49 Ford. Sunday mornings, her mother and father, her fiancé's mother and father, she, her brother and I would go bowling. All was in order while she waited for her husband-to-be. Her family and I pretty much occupied her time until his return.

One day, my first honest-to-goodness oldest best friend, Billy showed up on my doorstep. My cousin Donna Dee had found him wandering the streets of San Diego after he had gotten out of the Navy. He didn't have a place to stay so my mother and I invited him to live with us. The day he arrived, I had planned to go for a ride with that very special friend. We all three went for that ride, a ride that

68

Me, Kathy, Bill, Kathy's sisterJudy

would change our lives forever. Billy wanted to rent a piano, and so off we went, my dream girl, my best friend and me. The clerk behind the counter at the piano store noticed the engagement ring and asked..."Which one of you is the lucky guy?" The lucky guy turned out not to be her fiancé, but my best friend. When their eyes met, it was all over. All over, that is, for the guy who gave her that ring, and me.

My friend Bill

Kathy would borrow the family car, now that she knew how to drive, and would come to my house to visit Bill. They would visit right there on the front porch. Of course, neither of them knew how I felt and I couldn't say anything to the two most important people in my life. Six months later, they were married. They asked me to be their best man twice. The second time was when they decided to do it all again in the Catholic Church. I am godfather to two of their three children.

That dream girl infatuation, that awkwardness, has long since disappeared. I treasure my two special friends above all others. We are still very much like family even after Bill died from a heart attack in 2006. There were over 400 people at his funeral. He was a leader in his church and very much loved and respected. I often think of him and wish I could give him a call and talk of ol' times....I do speak with him, but not on the phone. I only wish he could answer me once in a while.

Before the Future
THE BLACK MIRACLE

Diane's senior prom

One of my pastimes for many years was roller-skating. It started when I was about fourteen years old. The Moonlight Roller Rink was the place to be every weekend. It became my social outlet and, without fail, I was there every Friday night and Sunday afternoon. Harry's Roller Rink was the next place I haunted, but the king of them all was where I met my first real love. The Hollywood

Roller Bowl was big and new and everyone was there, including Diane.

Diane

I was twenty-one and a decent skater. I had developed somewhat of a personality. Even though I had come out of my shell, I was still very awkward with girls. Up to this point I hadn't had anywhere near the experience of my friends. The only way I could impress a girl was to make her laugh. Diane was very pretty and had a great personality and a wonderful smile. She was the most popular girl at the Hollywood Roller Bowl. Her mother would bring her and sit there visiting with us. She also had a great personality and was easy to talk to. I, along with all the other young men, would do our best to hold Diane's attention. I got my share of chances but of course I wanted her all to myself. Somehow through some black miracle this happened, but for only four months.

One night, Diane didn't show up at the rink. I asked her girlfriend where she was. She told me "Diane isn't going to be coming any longer." My heart sank. Her girlfriend asked, "Are you Ron?" I said, "Yes." "Diane told me if I saw you to give you her number". Wow, I couldn't believe it. She chose me out of all those other guys!

On our first date, we doubled with Bill and Kathy. We wound up at Westlake Park (renamed MacArthur Park) and rented a boat. There on the water with the moon bright above we kissed for the first time. She looked at me with puzzled eyes and said, "No one has ever kissed me like that before"...I told her I had never kissed anyone I was in love with before.

We saw each other constantly and spent hours on the phone. I took her to her high school prom and gave her a friendship ring, which caused my world to crumble. Her father turned out to be extremely prejudiced. My skin was darker than Diane's. He said that ever since my mother and I attended a Mother's Day celebration with their family he was being shunned by family members. The ring set him off thinking the next step would be marriage.

The following Monday a note was left on my car at my work telling me to

The kiss at MacArthur Park

come right over after I got off. When I got to their home both Diane and her mother were crying. They told me the bad news that Andy, Diana's father, didn't want to face me for fear of making the situation worse. I left not quite knowing how this could happen. I drove home through a flood of tears. I couldn't sleep the rest of the night. All I kept asking was…why?

I found myself on her doorstep the next morning. When the door opened Diane's mother greeted me with open arms as though nothing happened. She was a wonderful lady. She was against the break-up and welcomed me in to hear me out. The three of us went to a priest and asked; then we went to their Lutheran minister and asked… why?

They both said that this was wrong and that they would pray for us. Diane and I tried to see each other on the sly, but her father had a much stronger hold on her. I once called and spoke to her mother asking where Diane was that day, and she said she had gone to Huntington Beach. I went looking for her and after many stops finally found her. I watched her playing volleyball with a group of friends then saw her give her phone number to a young man. She had always wanted a horse, so her father bought her one to distract her from me. Eventually he won and I suffered for two years before I could go to sleep without crying. Ironically, Diane's fathers' favorite song was *"As Time Goes By," "It's still the same old story, a fight for love and glory, the world will always welcome lovers, as time goes by…"* well, you know the rest.

Before the Future
TWO SWINGING GUYS
AND AN AMERICAN CRISIS

THE OLDEST DAILY NEWSPAPER IN THE UNITED STATES—FOUNDED 1771

The Philadelphia Inquirer
PUBLIC LEDGER
AN INDEPENDENT NEWSPAPER FOR ALL THE PEOPLE

FINAL
CITY EDITION

Kennedy Orders Cuba Blockade,
Calls Island Soviet Missile Base;
Navy to Sink Defiant Red Vessels

Bristol Girl Is Strangled In Choir Loft

Program of Action

40 Warships, 20,000 Men Start Siege

President Cites Kremlin Deceit In Atom Buildup

The Cuban Crisis of 1962 set the stage for someone who helped to comfort me in those years and many years since, Mark Jason. We met at the place I was working when I got that fateful note from Diane. Mark and I were drawn together through common passions, music and humor. During our late shift at Arrowhead and Purites Waters Company, we would sing at the top of our lungs. We were assigned to a special project because there was panic of water and food shortages should the Soviet Union launch missiles from nearby Cuba. Our company developed special ½ gallon cardboard cartons with plastic liners, to meet the needs of the public in the greater Los Angeles area.

Mark and I were assigned to work with an experimental machine that produced these special cartons. This new way of packaging water was located in the basement of the facility, which made for great acoustics for our singing. To while away the long hours we invented new songs, one of which was the infamous "Arrowhead Song" and so many others. It would be impossible to list them all. Mark was mischievous and full of energy. He saw the funny side of life and always had a plan to foil the system. I took to him right away. He was a free spirit ruled by the passion of life. We survived those few years at Arrowhead and eventually became roommates over on the West Side. I had introduced Mark to the rest of my friends. We all had great times at the beach or at our annual baseball picnics. We sang while Mark played his guitar. Mark sang, too, but he always wished he could sing like me. I always wished I could play the guitar like him.

Mark

There we were, two swinging bachelors living in a cool pad ready to bring on the girls, and we did. Sometimes we would have a couple of girls over for dinner, giving us a chance to show off our culinary skills. We tried to out-do each other by making the best, juiciest hamburgers. One time we got so carried away by adding too many ingredients in those award-winning hamburgers. When we tried to take them off the grill, they simply fell apart. We developed a signal to alert the other if we wanted our privacy. A small piece of paper was placed under the nameplate on the door. I came home one night and there it was. It was cold and late, so I crawled into the back seat of my car and covered myself with newspapers. There was a tap, tap, tap on the window about 3am. It was Mark. "It's okay, the coast is clear."

A girl I had been seeing asked if she could fix her girlfriend up with my roommate. I said, sure. When they arrived, I heard laughter just outside the door, then a knock. Our name tag on the door had sparked an uncontrollable giggle from the unknown guest.

When I opened the door, I saw who was doing the laughing and stumbled back in shock. I fell against a barstool and landed on the floor with my mouth open in disbelief. It was my old girlfriend from high school. The one I had dumped because of that dream. Mark, hearing the thud as I hit the floor, came rushing out and asked, "What happened?" As I climbed to my feet still unable to speak, the girls were laughing in hysteria. The first words out of my mouth were, "I'm sorry!" I tried to explain but she stopped me and said it was no big deal. She said she had long forgotten me and had already been through a divorce. "It's O.K. It's O.K." I really never had to tell her why. I was still feeling very awkward about the whole thing and refused to let Mark date my ex-girl friend, who I had so cold-heartedly dumped eight years before.

New Year's Eve 1965: Mark and I threw a party to end all parties. In our small one bedroom apartment, we packed in nearly eighty-five guests plus a three-piece band. Our eighty fifth guest left early but while she was there, she stole the show. She was our eighty-seven year-old downstairs neighbor. While she and a friend were having tea on her patio below, I had lowered a note down to her inviting her to our bash. The next day after coming home from work we found a small burlap bag tied to our doorknob. In the bag was a small bottle of booze and a note that read, "I would gladly attend your gala event." The night of the party I went downstairs to get her. She asked if her roommate, George, could come. She was referring to her cane. I don't remember her name, but she charmed everyone who spoke with her. I had the place decorated with streamers hanging from the ceiling about every square foot. When she walked into our

77

apartment her eyes lit up. As she looked around, she exclaimed, "It's like in the movies".

After her husband died and her three children had finished college and moved on, she took up sculpturing.

At the young age of sixty-five, she became quite famous as an artist. Several of her sculptures were featured at the Los Angeles County Museum of Art.

As we gathered around, she told stories of her travels to exotic places and the famous people she had met. I think we wore her out with so much attention besides, it was eight-thirty and well past her bedtime. We escorted her to her home and wished her and her roommate, George, a happy new-year. The guests now started to arrive by the dozens. We stuffed the band in the corner and they entertained us through the night. Bill even got up and did a magic show while the band took a break. We laughed, we danced, we sang and just had a great time. The party was a complete success.

Honored Guest

A story that Mark never lets me forget is when I told him his hamster died. I had put the message on a tape recorder with a note to "push play." I guess it was pretty cold not telling him in person. He has never forgiven me for that, but perhaps one day he will. After our year lease was up, Mark and I went our separate ways for a while. I went off to El Camino College then on to The Art Center and Mark went off to Malibu to live among the sorta rich and sorta famous.

❖

Before the Future
I'M RIGHT BEHIND YOU

PFC Ron   PFC George

It was 1963, and toward the beginning of the Viet Nam campaign. My old buddy George said we might be sent off to war. He said we had better join the reserves so we wouldn't get drafted. We did. There I was, in the U.S. Army Reserves. I never would have joined on my own. I was following George again, this time right into battle. The only real battle was to defeat feelings of being away from home. Being in the military takes all your personal life and tosses it out the window. "You're in the army now and not behind a plow.".... as the song goes. The physical challenges weren't near what I thought they might be. At twenty-three George and I were among the oldest

I'm on the far right then to my left, Bob then Fred

recruits in our unit. Most were eighteen or nineteen, some fresh out of high school.

When we arrived at Fort Ord, the bus pulled up to a line of drill instructors with shiny chrome helmets, starched uniforms and attitude. We got our first look at the real Army. As we stepped off of the bus with our long hair and civilian clothes, the shiny helmeted soldiers started to yell at the top of their lungs giving us orders to fall-in alphabetically. The D.I., who was yelling the loudest turned out to be my drill instructor. Lucky me.

One of the drill instructors ordered us to get in line to have our pictures taken. His exact words were, "Fall in, mens. Your goin' to get your pictures tooked." At that moment I felt as though we had left civilization behind.

George and I were separated at this point, and I was not to see him for several days. I was in the second platoon, and he was in the third. We spent the next six weeks in basic training and, to this day when I look at the group picture of the second platoon, I remember every one of those guys like it was yesterday. They were from all over the United States. We had a gambler who actually managed to bring a miniature roulette wheel with him. We called him Fats. He was fat. There was a black guy named Clayborn who would jump out of the second story window just because we asked him to. He also kept us up at night telling jokes. "Go to sleep, Clayborn!" A real character.

There was a guy who never took a shower. After a long march, he had the disgusting habit of biting his toenails. Several of us eventually had to give him a G.I. shower rubbing him raw with a stiff brush. A full-blooded Cherokee American Indian was in the bunk next to me. Enos was the toughest, meanest, best soldier in the whole darn company and fortunately he became a good friend. Then there was the bed wetter/cry baby. He slept in the bunk below me. Besides wetting his bed he would cry for his mother in his sleep. This poor guy also couldn't keep in step. He happened to march in front of me. When he got out of step the D.I. would tell me to kick him. When I didn't, Enos would run up from behind us, take my place and started doing the kicking. This guy was making Enos get out of step, too.

I became very close with a couple of guys, Bob Eastman and Fred Cahn. Bob was a laid back, easygoing person who always had a smile on his face. Fred was an urbanite from San Francisco. He was a budding artist and quite good. On our weekends off, I spent equal amounts of time with either Bob or Fred and their families. Fred was Jewish, which until then, was a culture I had not yet known. It was my first exposure to their family traditions. Each Saturday morning, Fred and his father would walk about six blocks to visit his grandmother. I went with them on those visits and enjoyed the way they met this old obligation with joy and love.

Bob lived south of San Francisco in a beautiful community with horse trails and narrow streets that wound through this out-of-the-way paradise known as Palo Alto. His family had some money but they lived a very simple life with no pretensions.

I kept in touch with these two friends over the years by telephone. One year I called Fred's house and to my shock found that he had died five months prior. He was in his early twenties when was taken by some strange disease.

Me in my Army fatigues

A very interesting event took place during our stay at basic training. Coincidentally, each one of our four platoons had a fat guy. During a relay race they wound up being the last to run, and our fat guy won. When we went on our final twenty-six mile march all the other fat guys quit, but our guy kept going. He came dragging into camp with the ambulance behind him. The rest of the company had already returned and half of us were finished with our showers. When someone spotted our brave fat guy coming down the trail, everyone in the whole company ran to the windows and cheered him on. It was a heroic effort. His reward was that none of his clothes fit after basic training. He had lost over forty-five pounds. We still called him Fats.

On that same twenty-six mile march, I had, in a small way, become a kind of hero. I always had a pack of LifeSavers handy to give me a little extra energy and to keep my mouth moist during those hot, dry marches. On the last leg of our march the company came to a halt and we were asked to raise our canteens over our heads and turn them upside down with the caps off. A recruit had fainted from exhaustion and desperately needed water. Out of some two hundred men, I was the only one who had any water left in my canteen. In fact, it was half full. The LifeSavers kept me from drinking my supply of precious water. My water gave that recruit what he needed to get back on the trail so on we marched, to become the welcoming committee for our soon-to-be hero who was bringing up the rear.

Sundays was a slow day, but we were encouraged to mop and polish the floor of the barracks. Not for me! I went to the Master Sergeant and requested a pass to go to choir practice at the campus church. Right away he was impressed that I would want to volunteer for such a noble task. My pass was granted, and I was off to church, leaving the menial chores to my fellow platoon mates. To my dismay, I wasn't needed at the church after all. So, now what? On my way back to my barracks, I passed the officer's club and thought, why not. I played pool with officers every Sunday from then on until basic training was over. Checking with the The Master Sergeant at the end of the day, he always gave me a welcoming smile, never knowing of my devious plan.

On our graduation from Basic Training, we were able to invite family and friends to witness our coming into manhood...full-fledged Army privates. I invited my family as well as a girl I had been dating and with whom I was quite serious. We would write several letters back and forth and, after bragging about her to my army buddies, they were all looking forward to meeting her. The day before our big event I received an eleven page "Dear Ron" letter. It took her those eleven pages to get to the point that she would not be coming and that it was over between us. I shined my boots over and over that day until the pain in my fingers distracted me from the pain in my heart.

The Army took me to a few places I might not have seen. One was Boston, another was Camp Lewis, Washington. Ironically, my grandfather, TaTa Al, carved on a walking stick, which I have in my possession, "February 19, 1918, Camp Lewis, Washington Company "A", 364th Inf." He had been there forty-seven years earlier. My grandfather received the Purple Heart while fighting the Germans in WWI. Purple Hearts were awarded to Army personnel who were wounded in action or who had been awarded the "Meritorious Services Citation Certificate" for service in World War I.

The Purple Heart awarded to my
grandfather TaTa Al

Before the Future

THE DAY THE WORLD STOOD STILL

1963...President John F. Kennedy was assassinated. Being on an army base at this time in history gives special meaning to this world tragedy. At Fort Ord, California over forty thousand men and women in uniform marched to a single rhythm toward the parade field. There wasn't a sound of cadence to be heard. All that could be heard was the sound of pant leg against pant leg as we all kept time like one giant heartbeat. There wasn't a soldier who wasn't in shock.

The light rain disguised the tears. I remember standing on that field, not feeling the cold or the discomfort as the hour passed while we honored our fallen leader.

I had a pass for that weekend and drove to San Francisco. There wasn't a soul around. The city was in mourning as was the rest of the world. I turned around and went back to camp to join my friends around the television to watch the memorable funeral procession. I can still hear that haunting drum beat as the president was taken to his final resting-place.

FOUND AND LOST...The Perfect Soul

After my tour of duty in the army, I worked for a while in an architectural office while attending school at night. I eventually had to enroll in daytime classes at El Camino College in order to qualify for my entrance into Art Center, my college goal. I was studying for my finals outdoors in the student eating area when I happened to see a girl about thirty feet away. I couldn't take my eyes off her. I couldn't concentrate on my studies any longer. I'm not sure I can describe her in words, because I was seeing her with my heart. My first vision of her was in profile. She had long brown hair, wore no make up and had a natural beauty that surrounded her like the glow of an angel. She had a softness about her that made me stare.

I found myself following her and her girlfriends into the student lounge. I sat about three tables away and looked at her over my book. I had to meet her, but how? What do I say? I wrote some thoughts on a small piece of paper. I tried to remember them, but when I started toward her table my mind went blank. I got about ten feet away, and my knees started to buckle. I broke out in a light sweat and started to shake. I turned back to my table. I got up again but returned to my table. I was now making it worse for myself. Then she stood up! She was leaving! I took a deep breath. I don't know how I got there, but I found myself at her table. I spoke. "Hi, I'm Ron. What's your name?" Of course, I had forgotten all I had written. "Hi, my name is Kristy Kilpatrick." "Oh nice to meet you." I walked away. What a jerk, I thought. I was still desperate.

I went to the student locator on campus and looked for her name and phone number. There it was. At the time, I was managing a fast food restaurant after school. As soon as I arrived, I called her from the telephone booth just outside my work. She answered. I apologized for my forwardness and more or less told her that I had followed her, then looked for her name and number in the student locator. She said that she uses it to find people herself and said it was Okay. After some small talk, I asked her out and she accepted. Needless to say I was on top of the world and could hardly wait to see her.

As we began to date, I found that she was very unhappy at home. She didn't get along with her mother at all, in fact, they were leaving notes to each other and not even speaking. I began to try to console her and give her comfort. We would talk and talk for hours trying to find ways to understand what was going wrong. I wanted her to be as happy as she made me. At the time, I was in the Army Reserves and was scheduled to go to my two-week summer camp. I was going to miss Kristy very much but I had to go.

While I was away, I waited for my letters to be answered…but nothing. I called her first thing when I returned home. Her mother answered and said…"Kristy no longer lives here." I asked. "Where is she?" Her mother told me that Kristy had gotten married and moved up north. My heart sank. I had to talk to her.

I called her girlfriend and asked. "What happened?" She told me in so many words, that I was acting too much like an uncle and not enough like a person with whom she could escape. This girl friend had introduced Kristy to someone who could give her the freedom she needed. In that short time I was away, he married her and took her away from her troubles, her mother and me. I was able to get in touch with Kristy and speak to her that day. She told me essentially the same thing her girlfriend had and that she felt very bad that she had to hurt me. I wished her well and was glad she was finally at peace. Obviously, I didn't realize the urgency of her predicament and I guess I wasn't really ready to make that kind of commitment.

I will always remember Kristy Kilpatrick. That inexplicable feeling I had when I first saw her. Her gracefulness when she first spoke to me and told me her name. The joy I felt when she agreed to go out with me. How she made me feel just being near her. The time she played the piano for me…"Summertime…hush little baby, don't you cry…"

THE PERFECT SOUL
I picked a Perfect Flower in a field of many
I drew it to my lips and became intoxicated by it's nectar
I caressed it and sang with my heart to it's loveliness
Slowly this beautiful flower began to lose it's petals
I tried in vain to replace them
but in the end this Perfect Flower was hiding a thorn that has
left me with a pain that will not die
I let go this Perfect Flower to the winds of time in hopes
that it's petals may find the Perfect Soul

WHAT'S THAT SMELL?

In order to afford my first semester at Art Center, I had to make a few sacrifices, one was to give up my little black book and the other was to sell my classic 1958 Porsche. I've had many cars in my lifetime but my Porsche was the best. The very day the new owner was to pick up the car, my old high school buddy, Pat Moran, begged me to let him drive my precious machine. Pat's reputation for challenging any car to a drag race had me worried. Pat was a good driver, but it seemed he was always going just a little faster than the next guy. On this memorable day, the final day of being the owner of a classic sports car, I finally gave in. He chose the windiest road he could find to test the car's abilities. I, of course, had never driven the car to its limits for fear of wrapping it around a pole. Pat, on the other hand, gave us the ride of our lives. He went into those curves like a demon, handling that car with confidence and daring. All I could do was hang on.

When he pulled over, we were both breathing hard, Pat from his efforts and me from absolute terror. He turned and looked at me and said, "That was bitchin'. " You gotta try it." So I did. It was the most exhilarating thing I had ever done. We pushed that car to the limits, going into power turns, skidding, and burning rubber at every turn. When we got back to my house to meet the new owner, the first thing he asked was, "What's that smell?" It was the smell of burning rubber! Of course, we made up some excuse about some old car that had just passed. I sold that dream car for $2,300.00. The same price I'd paid for it one year previous. In 1997 the same car could be had for ten times that amount. Giving up the Porsche was torture, but I couldn't afford the payments and attend college. The little black book I gave up was a must. There was now absolutely no time for an active social life.

GOING INTO BATTLE
AND FINDING PEACE

Art Center College campus on West 3rd Street circa 1960

Art Center was extremely demanding. At least four hours of homework each night, including weekends. All nighters each week was not uncommon. Our classes were from 9am to 4pm daily. Because I hadn't finished my academic requirements I had to take those classes on Saturdays plus two evenings. My plate was indeed full.

Even though it was tremendously demanding there was a kind of peace about the campus. We were all there because we shared a common bond. We all loved design and the arts. I hadn't really been able to share these feelings with my high school friends. I now felt at

93

home and at ease with this bunch of strangers from all over the world. There were over fifteen states and seven countries represented and each of us had a passion for learning as much as we could about the professional arts. The first two semesters were dedicated to the basics.

We were told to forget everything we had learned about art and design because we were going to be taught the correct way. It was like going into battle. All of us grew closer and closer with one common goal, to get though the semester. We helped each other when we could, but most of the time it was one against the other. The whole premise was, as we were to learn, total competition. Unlike the academic world, our assignments were displayed in front of the entire class for criticism. Otherwise known as "the crit." After that first crit the nights got longer. Your concept could always be improved. Time was always the enemy.

Some instructors were kind, but most were blatantly honest. After all, they were paid to mold us into great designers, or at least give us the chance to prove ourselves or fail. Most students did well but some probably shouldn't have been admitted in the first place. The ones who survived those first two grueling semesters were either exceptional or were motivated by desire and time. For the ones of us who were in our middle to late twenties, time was running out. We had to make this work.

After that second semester in June of 68' a small group of us decided to go backpacking into the high Sierras…(Barney, Steve, Gary, Dennis, Per, and me.) We had only known each other a short time but we had survived thirty-four weeks of basic training. I had never done any serious backpacking before and had no camping gear at all. My backpack was thrown together with bits and pieces of other equipment. As we set out on our trek, everyone had some sort of man-toy. Two guys had fishing poles, one guy had a large hunting knife, a couple of others had their 35mm cameras and one even brought a pistol. I was the only one who didn't have a toy so when we stopped in Bishop for supplies, I found my man-toy. I was now the proud new owner of a serious slingshot.

The site where we saw an amazing fish story unfold

The trip up the mountain was the most physically challenging thing I'd done in a long time. I happened to be the old man of the group at twenty-seven. We were following a mule trail, with switchbacks, at an unbelievable incline. I actually needed help on the last leg of our ascent. My legs just wouldn't work any longer. After seven hours we finally leveled out and decided on a campsite. It was absolutely beautiful up there. We made camp next to a stream with un-melted snow ice, still there from the past winter. There was a large lake just a couple hundred feet away.

The next day, we each decided to explore our own interests. I chose to stay close to camp, simply enjoying the quiet and the peace, until I saw my opportunity to use my toy. A small bird landed in the brush about thirty feet away. I took aim and let go a small steel ball with my serious slingshot. To my amazement, I hit the poor little thing. I rushed over to find it was very dead. I buried the beautiful little bird, paused for a few minutes, then stood up and threw that serious slingshot man toy as far into the forest as I could. The rest of the day I lay on a rock out on the lake, trying to bring peace back into my soul.

Another day, we hiked the John Muir Trail and stopped at a pond to do some fishing, we witnessed an incredible fish story in the making. One of the guys had caught a small trout and was slowly reeling it in. To our amazement, an even bigger trout was nipping at the tail of the smaller trout. When the big fish bit into the small fish both were quickly yanked ashore. They were delicious. We caught our limit every day.

It was time to head back. After seven days on the mountain, we were ready. Well-rested and with empty packs, we were able to run most of the way. The trip down only took forty-five minutes. Home at last. I jumped into a welcoming bath and soaked. While drying, I felt what felt like loose skin in the small of my back. I reached around and pulled. To my horror I was holding a large wood tick still wiggling in my fingers. I quickly threw it into the toilet and when inspecting my back again, there was a second creature dining on my back.

Ray Bradbury

After that trip we each found other interests to occupy our time between semesters. Still it was one of my most memorable semester breaks.I graduated from Art Center in 1970, and our guest speaker that year was Sci-fi writer, Ray Bradbury. I had read several of his books and was very honored when he shook my hand congratulating me upon my graduation.

❖

LOST IN HELL FOR SEVEN DAYS

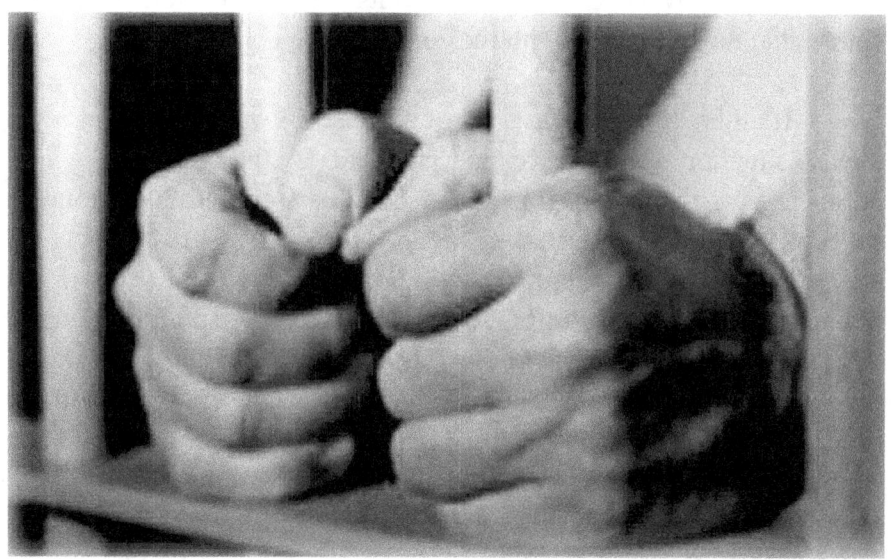

Towards the end of my sixth semester something very unexpected happened to me. I was falsely arrested and lost in jail for seven days.

It was Sunday morning, about 2:30am. I was working on my final assignment for the semester and had anticipated working through the night. I decided to take a break and get something to eat so I drove to the all-night market just ten minutes away. On the way back, I took a couple side streets through an industrial area and, as I approached the main street, I was interrupted by a squad car. It pulled directly in front of me, so I couldn't proceed into the intersection. Just then another police car pulled along side of me heading in the opposite direction. Two officers jumped out of the car with their weapons drawn and yelled at me to step out of my car with my hands clear. At the time, my car was in the shop and I was driving a loaner car and when they asked for the key to the trunk I explained that it wasn't my car and didn't have the key to the trunk. One of the policeman pried open the trunk with a screwdriver and found a crowbar which he grabbed and shook it at me saying, "Is this what you used to break into the building?", in shock, I said, "First of all, there is no key, and second, you now have your fingerprints all over the crowbar." Of course that didn't sit well with the cops.

It all happened so fast. All of a sudden, I was the subject of an intense situation. I did exactly as I was told. By the time I had gotten out of my car there were four more squad cars around me, a total of six black-and-whites were at the scene. Apparently, there had been an attempted break-in at one of the warehouses nearby, and I was in the wrong place at the wrong time. After a lot of on-the-spot questioning, I was read my rights and carted off to jail. I kept telling them that if they went to my apartment they would see that I had left my paint brush still full of paint, with the lights on and the radio going. They would see they had the wrong guy. They didn't seem to be listening and off I went.

It was nearly 3:30am by the time we got to the station. The officer sitting behind a typewriter asked..."What have you got there?" "Burglary." "Shoulda' shot him", the officer said. I was granted my one phone call but I asked if I could make it in the morning. It seemed too late to call anyone, especially my mother who at the time was very ill with diabetes.

I was worried she might have a reaction if she heard my bad news. It seemed that they were pretty serious about keeping me for a while, so my first real concern was to get in touch with my army reserve unit. I was due for a reserve meeting the coming weekend and had already missed my allotted two meetings. The third miss was always a threat to be sent to active duty to Viet Nam. I couldn't talk to them until the next day anyway so it was another reason I chose to

Cell block. Los Angeles County Jail

delay my phone call. I would then ask them to get in touch with someone to get me out of this place.

As fate would have it, when morning rolled around at about 6am, there was a shift change, and the new officer on duty didn't believe I hadn't made my allotted call. I was denied my phone call. There I was, stuck with no one knowing where I was.

I was then taken to an arraignment court with many others and had a chance to speak with a public defender. He, after hearing my story, assured me I could be released on my own recognizance. When I got before the judge she read my case and asked how I would plead. I said, "not guilty" and proceeded to ask for being released on my own recognizance. Before I could finish my sentence, she said, "Next case." I was firmly escorted out of the courtroom into a holding room.

I was taken to a processing center where I was to be issued jail clothes and bedding. My personal belongings were taken from me and put in a small metal box with a number on it, my number. I got the clothes but they were fresh out of bedding and mattresses. I had to sleep on the cold, hard concrete floor with nothing to cover myself and woke up the next morning with a cold. I asked to go to the infirmary, and got in line. I had also asked if I could send a telegram which I understood was the only other outside contact allowed. While in the infirmary, I saw an officer in the hall through the window in the door, so I opened the door to ask where I could send a telegram. He grabbed me by my collar and shoved me into the infirmary room, where I fell backwards onto the floor in front of about twenty others. I was now at a new low, wondering if I would ever get out.

After returning to the cell area, my name was called out along with about thirty others. We were then transferred to another facility on those black and white sheriff buses with bars on the windows. These same buses I'd seen many times, wondering who was inside. This new place gave me a very uneasy feeling. It was old and it smelled! I began to notice that my traveling companions looked very hardened. I then realized this transfer was to a felony unit. I was now very fearful of what might happen. We were assigned two each to three-man cells, which were already full. This meant we had to sleep outside the cell on the floor in a row stretching the length of the thirty-cell block.

I happened to be toward the end, where there were a number of blacks. One young black man came from the opposite end of the block and told a white man next to me that he wanted to trade places with him. He told the white guy to be gone by the time he got back with his gear. When he returned, the white man was on his hands and knees, still picking up his bedding. The black man shouted at him. "I thought I told you I wanted you to be gone when I got back." With that the black man, from a standing position, came up with a full uppercut punch hitting the white man in the neck. He fell forward onto his face and didn't move. There was a commotion, and suddenly we found ourselves locked in the cells. The guards were going to each cell and randomly pulling out black men and taking them away. They then came with a stretcher and took the man who had been hit away. As they passed the cell I was in, I could see they had covered his head. The blow had killed him.

I then noticed that I was in a cell with five blacks. One of them started boasting how he had put that white boy away. There I was in the same cell with the killer. I just stood there grabbing the bars and held on tight. As far as I knew, they never did find the right person. I was not sure exactly who it was. I didn't want to look any of the blacks in the eye. I could only think of getting out. The blacks were all very high on the event and were talking of their past adventures in the streets, each in turn giving graphic accounts of their actions, all of which were very ugly.

I finally had a chance to speak with a priest who apparently was able to get a telegram out for me. I waited, but never heard from him. Finally, on the seventh day, I was told I had a visitor. Pat Moran, my old high school buddy, had not heard from me in a while. He started calling hospitals, and friends, and eventually the city jail. He posted my bail, and I was free. It felt like I had been away for a lifetime.

It wasn't over yet. I first had to pay $38.00 to get the my out of impound which, to a poor student in 1967, was a lot of money. When I got back to my apartment everything was still as I had left it. Of course the paint in my brush had dried and the assignment, was still unfinished. By this time, the semester was over, school was essentially closed for two weeks. When I returned to the instructor to explain my reason for not turning in the assignment he took a very unexpected attitude, professing not to believe me. Then he said that it was too late anyway to do anything about it, and said my grade was already in process. He gave me a letter grade of 'D' for the semester. The class was a lettering class. Ironically, ten years later I taught that same class at a community college and received excellent reviews from both my students and the dean of design.

I now had to deal with the United States Army Reserves. At my next meeting I had to go before the commanding officer, who happened to be a replacement. My original C.O. was a real nice guy. This replacement wasn't so nice. He had a nickname, which had followed him to our unit...No Neck. He looked the part. He was short and had no neck, just a very large head sitting on top of a squatty little body. Next to his head was a sizable chip on his shoulder. He, too, didn't believe my story. The only way I could convince him was to go back to the arresting officer and get written proof of my internment. That in itself was a humiliating experience.

One other little mishap I should mention here. After returning the loaner and picking up my car as I was driving home, the engine blew up.

Before the Future
CHEESECAKE AND THE RAIN

13 Part VI—Thurs, Apr 9, 1970   Los Angeles Times

BALANCE—Wine being poured for Wendy Vanguard, lends elegance to simple, inexpensive meal of French toast and bacon, cooked by artist Ronald Crosthwaite.

Student Brings a Pragmatic Approach to Menu Problems

I survived that horrible ordeal and was ready for the next semester. Things had to get better. And they did. My studies were at an all time high. One day, while I was sitting in the cafeteria, minding my own business, this nice looking lady in a business suit came up to me and asked, "Can you cook? Are you married? Do you have any special dishes you've prepared?" The answers I gave to her were yes, no, and yes. Naturally she was interested. She said, "Are you free next Tuesday at about 4pm?" I said, "I guess so," not knowing what was going on. She then introduced herself as the Public Relations Director at the school for which she was doing an article about single bachelor students who could cook. "Can you make it?" I said, "Sure." "Fine," she said. "I'll be there with a reporter and a photographer from the Los Angeles Times to do an on-the-spot interview with you." She said it would be a nice touch if "maybe you had a young lady to share the spotlight." I agreed. It all seemed to happen so fast, but why not.

I prepared my special Orange French Toast. It was something I had made on the spot one day for some friends who dropped in. Their reaction was..."mmmmm." Served with Japanese plumb wine... voila! There I was, in the L.A. Times' Thursday food section with photo, interview, and recipes. I shared my fame with a girl to whom I had been attracted but had avoided for a very long time because I new she would get to me. She was someone I had spotted the very first semester, but I wasn't alone. She always had admirers surrounding her. It took me about three semesters before I too was part of her following.

Wendy and I dated from time to time, but I was always on the defensive. I had my reasons for being cautious. We'd had some very special moments, but she always managed to keep me at bay, for which I'm very grateful. New York cheesecake and the rain will always remind me of Wendy. I told her that one

Happy Ron

day she would love me. She didn't quite know how to react. Sometime after we graduated, she said, "If we were to get married, how would you feel if I kept my last name?" At the time, I didn't know why she would want to keep her name after marrying me. I probably said something philosophical, trying not to act too shocked.

Of course nothing happened as a result. I know now that what Wendy was trying to say. She wanted to keep her identity while pursuing her career as an artist.

After graduation, our instructor, the head of the environmental department, hired my best friend, Gaylord, and me. He was the kind of instructor we all admired. He always gave us very challenging and interesting projects. There I was working, for him. When he asked if I could recommend someone to do some graphic work, I introduced him to Wendy. Little did I know that, years later, when Wendy and I were having tea and cheese cake one afternoon, she tells me she'd had an affair with my boss. My Wendy and my boss!? She *did* say he was lousy in bed. Oh, that made me feel a lot better. Another bubble popped...

By this time, Wendy had gotten married and was two months pregnant. She and her husband, one of her more serious followers, asked if I would design their new office. I did. Only through the electronic world did Wendy and I met up once again. She invited me to a jazz concert in Pasadena. Seeing her after thirty-five years was pretty special. That night after the show, we closed a local restaurant talking for hours, catching up. I haven't seen or heard from her since.

Several years later, I featured a photo of Wendy and me on the cover of my current book, "The Undone".

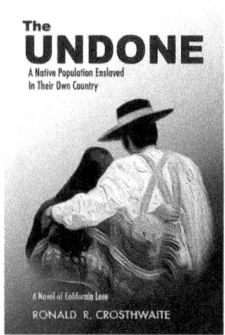

Before the Future
THE STUDIO GANG

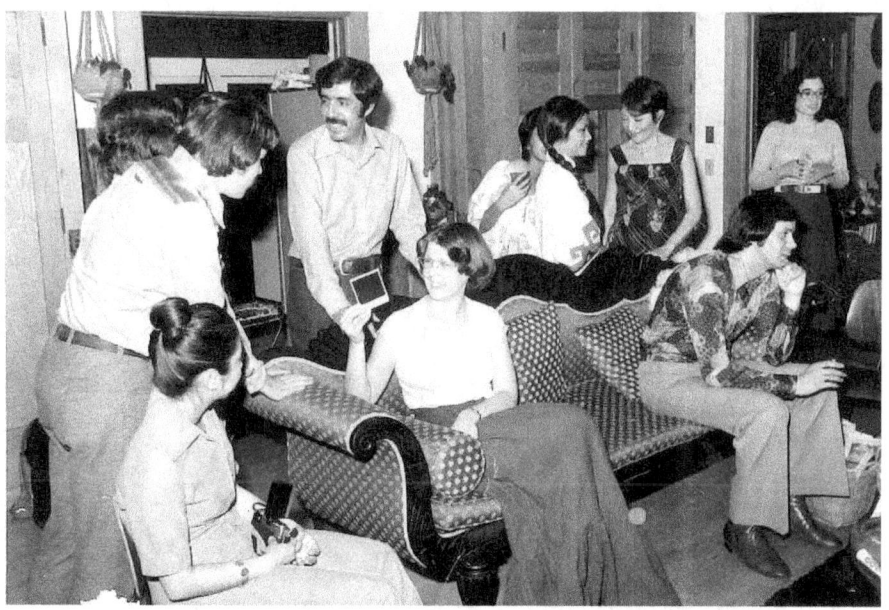

The Studio Gang. Hollis Cotton, Tony Palazzola ,Per Volquartz, Bron Smith, Don Munz and me

A little over two years after I graduated from Art Center, a classmate asked me to come work with him. It turns out that several Art Center graduates shared a studio in Pasadena at a storefront space on Garfield Street. I became a part of that group. We started out trying to break into the graphic world by doing a lot of promotional work. We had all worked together in the graphic department at the Barry Berkus office in West L.A., Norm Inouye, Tony Palazzola, Don Munz, and me. We thought, "here we go"… but it didn't take. We eventually struck up a relationship with another group of guys from Art Center. They were sharing a very large house in the path of the Long Beach Freeway. The State now owned the house, as well as many others in the area, which made the rent very attractive.

107

Dr. Cotton owned the house, but when the State took over, his son Hollis moved in and the studio began. Hollis had gone to Arizona State College to study architecture, but wound up at Art Center in the Advertising Department where he met Per Volquartz. Per, a product of the Danish discipline, was a 'hero' in the eyes of the school. In the many years I've known Per he has never had to work for anyone. He has always been his own boss. Per is many things; photographer, graphic designer, illustrator, cartoonist, animator, and computer whiz. Above all he was a gracious and giving friend. He came to this country with hardly any money and an over abundance of talent. The first time I met Per was on the semester break when we all went backpacking. When we picked him up, he was eating corn flakes with water. The poor guy couldn't even afford milk.

Per Volquartz

He had proven himself to be a stiff competitor in the world of design and business. In his later years, Per literally took the place of the famous nature photographer, Ansel Adams, taking students to field trips as Ansel had done, giving them the benefit of his knowledge of nature photography. Per himself took the last of Ansel Adams' seminars to the High Sierras before his death.

Hollis Cotton played an important role in my becoming interested in my family history. He asked me to be his main subject in a student film being shot in Baja California. I was to play a priest just out of seminary, starting my first job. Hollis told me in Baja the name Crosthwaite was quite well known, and he was sure I might be related to them. We had to retrieve the key to a small church nestled out in a cornfield. It just so happened the key to the church was held by the owner of a local grocery store who's name was Crosthwaite. When I was introduced she immediately asked me, in a very thick Spanish accent, "Are you one of *the* Crosthwaite's?" I didn't know if I was or not. She proceeded to tell me about who I might be and, sure enough, she named names which were familiar, I *was* one of those Crosthwaite's. This sparked an interest that wasn't to be acted upon until fourteen years later, after I had searched for my father and found him. He and his father before him, had been doing family research, and I simply picked up where they left off.

Bron Smith

Bron Smith was another of the studio gang who had his own distinct brand of talent and character. I say character with true validation. Bron was a cartoon come to life. As a cartoonist, he seemed to take on every characteristic of his subjects. He could keep us in stitches either with the off-brand of humor or sound effects only he could make: the sound of a dripping faucet or his double whistle. He seemed to always step into humorous situations when it came to sex. He is a devout Christian and was constantly defending his innocence, but managed to entertain us with his excuses while fumbling for an answer. One of the funniest lunches I think I have ever tried to get through was the time Per, Bron, Dee, and I were discussing the value of fruit. Dee was a perky little Japanese girl we befriended who would come to our studio for lunch.

One time, oranges was the topic of discussion. It seemed that Bron had made reference to oranges as an analogy to breast size, referring to Dee quite by accident, or so he led us to

109

believe. Dee jumped right in and kept asking leading questions causing Bron to fall all over himself. Bron, being a devout Christian, tried desperately to protect his virtue. To this day the very mention of oranges in the presence of Per or Dee takes us back to the uncontrollable laughter we all shared during that afternoon lunch.

Tony Palazzola was the one who originally called me to help with a project involving Dr. Cotton. Hollis contracted a four story medical center for his step–father, James Spear. Hollis had Tony do the interior design. I was called in to help with the space planning. Tony and I worked on the project for almost two years and hardly made any money. I stuck it out another two years while Tony tried to bring more work for us. We had some success, but eventually it was time to move on.

Don Munz, the senior member of the group, had more energy and enthusiasm than all of us put together. Don was a full-time teacher at Pasadena Community College. He shared our studio while creating his newly designed graphic originals. He also needed a space to conduct his after hours classes. A couple times a week Don would bring in a group of students to learn all that they could from the master. Don also

Don Munz

had some of the same problems Professor Indiana Jones had, keeping the young ladies at bay. I'd say Don had the look of Sean Connery and the charm of Maurice Chevalier; an irresistible combination for some students. Come to think of it, I don't remember ever seeing a single male student in those after hours classes. Dons' passion was his love for the printed serigraph. To our surprise, he decided to give up teaching and go to the East Coast to become a bohemian. He wanted to follow his passion to become a fine artist and make his contribution to 'The World According to Don Munz.'

We gave him a going away party to end all going away parties. Don loved mayonnaise, so all who attended the party were asked to bring mayonnaise. We had every size and variety of the white stuff you could imagine. The crowd consisted of many of his students and all of his friends.

As a result of Don's leaving the teaching business, those of us who wanted took over his classes. We divided them up among us and kept our studio jobs. This launched my teaching career. I taught lettering and two-dimensional design. Some classes were held in the morning and others were in the evening.

Teaching graphic design at Pasadena Community College

I was so nervous that first morning in the lettering class that my knees were actually giving out on me. I had to prop myself up against the desk in order not to fall over. I eventually got the hang of it and was really into it. A few years later, one of my students came to work for me. I asked her if I seemed to be nervous when introducing myself to my first class. She hadn't seen any sign of that. I think just talking about myself and what I had accomplished in my professional life had put me at ease.

Through the year, one class stands out as one of my proudest moments. I had a quadriplegic student in my beginning design class. I was known for not letting any one out of my class unless they'd learned and produced actual artwork. This student was to become my ultimate challenge. I was able to show him how to get results from direct approach applications. His hands were very distorted, but I showed him that if he pushed the brush into the back of his hand and gripped tightly he could control the stroke by smashing the brush down against the surface of the illustration board. It worked. When I held his efforts up to the class, all his classmates became inspired to do better work.

My evening classes had their own kind of specialty. Most of these students were changing careers and were more motivated to learn. I always had a radio playing classical music in the background. One student would bring snacks to share with everyone. She, along with several other of my students, stayed in touch with me and would come to my annual baseball picnics. Every semester on the last day of the class, it was party time.

At some of the semesters' last day, I would invite my students who had children to bring them to the party. My intention was to have the children do the final crit. The assignment was to abstractly depict animals or insects on each side of a six-inch cube they had constructed. The children were right on. After the final crit, that night, no one wanted to leave. But of course, all good things must end but can stay with you as a fruitful memory. I believe they went away with an understanding of the concept of basic design. Many of them would come back after going on to Art Center to have me look at their work. It was the highest compliment I could have imagined...I miss teaching.

The studio years were among some of my most memorable in the industry. Besides working with a bunch of creative and great guys we would throw these great New Year's Eve parties. They were more like food feasts. We, as a variety of nationalities, brought food from all over the world. One large room was set aside as the food orgy room. Wall to wall food. There was Italian, Chinese, Japanese, Filipino, Danish, Mexican, and American, just to name a few.

I would put together taped music with sound effects thrown in for flavor. We would play games, sing and, do skits. One year we had my mother's landlord, Lou Casas, call a square dance. It was great fun. At every opportunity, we would throw a party. We all had lots of friends and would always fill the place to capacity.

Per is the only one who occupied the studio after we broke up. All had moved on. We got together again to celebrate Per's fiftieth birthday. He was just twenty when I'd first met him, eating that bowl of Cornflakes with water…It's been a long road. When we lost Per, too early, there were many of his former students and followers giving testimony after testimony at his memorial. Per had inspired us all.

Before the Future
A CRY FOR HELP

Early one evening, I was getting ready for a first date when there was a knock at my door. It was a girl who lived a few apartments away. She asked if she could come in and talk. I said, "Okay, but I'm on my way out very soon." She had a bundle of keys in one hand and a drink in the other.

She seemed a little out of it when she started talking about a whole lot of nothing. The drink was taking over. She asked to use the bathroom. It was a reasonable request, but when she stayed in there a little longer than normal, I knocked. "Are you all right?" I heard what sounded like giggling and crying at the same time. I opened the door and found her staring at her reflection in the mirror with tears streaming down her cheeks, with streaks of dark mascara lining her face. She kept saying over and over, "I did it. I finally did it." At the same time, I noticed the razor in her hand and blood gushing from her left wrist. I reached out very slowly and plucked the razor from her hand and threw it into the bedroom. In the same motion grabbed a towel and wrapped it around her wound. The towel happened to be a bright red Christmas towel handed down to me by my mother. There was no way to tell how much was blood and how much was towel. I held onto her arms and started pulling and dragging her toward the kitchen, trying to keep her off the carpet. She was bleeding pretty badly, and I wasn't about to let the carpet get it.

She was fighting me the whole way screaming, "No, no, they'll take him away. No, no" I managed to wrestle her to the floor, I had to sit on her to contain her. She kept bucking up and down while I tried to call for help. It was all I could do to hang on. I've never hit a girl in my life, but the time had come. With one swift slap to her face, her wig flew across the room. She was quiet and just stared at me as I completed my dialing. (At this time in history, all we had was dial phones. Cell phones hadn't been invented, and touch-tone phones were on the horizon.) Within minutes, three large uniformed firemen were crashing through my screen door. As they took over, the girl glared at me and said, "I'll never forgive you for this." I asked the one holding her, "Did I do the right thing?" He assured me I had, and they were gone.

She was off to UCLA Medical Emergency. I quickly called my date. "You'll never guess what happened," I exclaimed. She was very understanding and said she'd be anxiously awaiting my arrival. Before I could leave, two L.A. policemen came to my door. They interrogated me as though I had committed a crime. They were rude and not at all understanding of the situation. Eventually, they seemed satisfied with my innocence and left. As I got myself back together and was about to leave, the phone rang. It was the ER doctor at the hospital. He asked if I could tell him the name of the girl just admitted for attempted suicide. I only knew her as Dora. I never knew her last name, I explained. He said it was imperative they had her identity and asked if there was any way I could help. I noticed her keys were still in my apartment and said, "I'll see what I can do."

I went into her apartment not knowing what to look for. Eventually, I came upon a letter addressed to her by her parents. The doctor was grateful to have the information, and now I could go on with my life. I was almost out the door again, and the phone rang once more. It was her. She said. "You gotta get me outta here, these people are crazy." She then asked me to bring her some articles in her overnight bag. I went back to her apartment and gathered her belongings, then rushed over to the hospital to find they had transferred her to a special holding clinic about four miles away.

Upon my arrival, I was greeted by two doctors who, in-turn, asked about the events that brought Dora to them. They wouldn't let me see her, but I heard her yell, "Get me outta a here." The doctors explained they were not able to get in touch with any of her family members, and they had no rooms for her at this facility. They were going to have to transfer her to Camarillo (at the time, Camarillo was a state psychiatric hospital) and admit her as attempted suicide which would jeopardize her being able to keep her son. That's what she was yelling about, her baby. It turns out her child was being cared for by her parents, but still legally awarded to her. The doctors said it's either Camarillo or she could be released to someone she knew…Guess who got the job? I had arranged to have my date meet me at the hospital so we could just go from wherever. Now I had to go out to her car and tell her the evening was over. Again, she was understanding and asked me to call her when things mellowed out.

As we drove away from the hospital, Dora told me she was in a lot of pain. After what she had done, no pain medicine would have been prescribed in order that the patient could experience the actual pain in hopes they wouldn't try it again. She pleaded with me to get her something for the pain. I gave in and pulled into the empty parking lot of an all night-market. I rushed out with the medicine and couldn't see her in the car. I panicked, but as I got closer, I found that she had slid down in her seat.

At my place we were both exhausted from the ordeal and went right to bed. I put her down on the couch, covered her with a blanket and went to my bedroom. I was about to fall asleep when I heard a noise coming from the other room. I ran to the kitchen to find Dora about to slash her other wrist with a knife. I grabbed the knife from her and got behind her holding onto both arms and walked her back to the living room. Not letting go, I pulled her onto the couch where we both soon fell into a deep sleep. We stayed that way through the night. I didn't dare let go of her.

We awoke the next morning to birds singing and a bright sunny day. I asked, "Are you all right?" She acted as though nothing had happened and told me she was feeling fine. It tried to give her the card one of the psychiatrists had given me to give to her, but she said, "They were all crazy", which had been her favorite expression. With that she was out the door and gone.

I did some chores and was listening to music when, about 3p.m., she was at my door again. "Would you mind taking me to the movies? There's a film some friends said I should see." I said, "Ah…. sure. What time?" As she walked away, she yelled out, "four-thirty." "What's the name of the movie?" She yelled back…"Play Misty for me."

I had no idea what I was in for. When the scene came of a woman who had just slit her wrists and was lying in her bathtub in a pool of blood, I slowly looked over at Dora and asked "Are you alright?" She just stared up at the screen from her slumped position.

For several weeks, I could not come home at night without getting a funny feeling in the pit of my stomach, thinking she might be waiting in the shadows for me. If you're not familiar with the movie, it has to do with the woman who had attempted suicide, then was saved by a neighbor whom she began to stalk, waiting in the shadows of his home when he would come home. She had become jealous of his former girlfriend and was bent on getting even.

One day, I found Dora in the yard playing with her son outside my apartment. She introduced me, and the next day was gone. One year passed before I was to hear from her. She called me, and said she was doing well, enrolled in school, and working. No questions about me, just reporting about herself. I was to get one more call still another year later. Essentially the same message, a report on how she was doing, I believe she was thanking me the only way she knew how.

Before the Future
ROYALTY COMES TO LOS ANGELES

And I Flew Twenty Feet

Their Majesties, the King and Queen of Spain, Don Juan Carlos I and Dona Sofia, arrived at the El Pueblo Historic Park on the 30th of September 1987 at 11:45 a.m. They were here to dedicate the statue of King Juan Carlos III who decreed the founding of El Pueblo de la Reina de Los Angeles on September 4, 1781.

Mayor Tom Bradley was then in office and offered a generous welcome to our distinguished guests. The City Council, along with an entourage of dignitaries, was in attendance. There was the brass quintet of Don Waldrop and dancers from Ballet Folklorico of La Fonda Los Cameros and the dance group Alegre. Later, at a Gala Dinner at the Museum of Contemporary Art, the music of the Monsignor Strings was performed.

The invitation that accompanied Their Majesties' photograph read:
The City of Los Angeles is deeply honored by the visit of Their Majesties The King and Queen of Spain, Don Juan Carlos I and Doña Sofia.

From a Pueblo settled by forty-four Pobladores (men, women, and children of Spanish, Indian and African ancestry), Los Angeles has enjoyed spectacular growth, which is a twentieth-century

Me in front of the Avila Adobe at Olvera Street
Antonio Avila was my grandmother's grandfather

phenomenon. The Pueblo, in just two centuries, has become a premier international city and the second- largest city in the United States. It was the vision of the courageous explorers from Christopher Columbus to Juan Rodriquez Cabrillo, Gaspar de Portola, Father Junipero Serra, Felipe de Neve and Father Crespi that led us to today's celebrations. The visit of their Majesties to Los Angeles was a delightful recognition of the ties that bind our two countries.

Me and Eddie Albert

While I was waiting for the arrival of the King and Queen, I spotted a personality from the silver screen; the one and only Eddie Albert. I boldly went up to Mr. Albert and asked if he wouldn't mind if I were to have a picture of the two of us together. He was very nice about it and said, "Sure." I asked why he was here at this celebration. He told me he took great interest in early California history because his wife, Margo, was a Mexican film actress. When I told him that I was a Pobladore, he was very interested in hearing my story. We chatted for a while until Father Mahoney sat down with him. He introduced me, and we all three talked about this great event.

Later that day was a scheduled visit to Olvera Street and the Avila Adobe, the oldest structure in Los Angeles. My families' ancestors had been the owners of this historic adobe. My mother's great, great, great-grandfather was Antonio Ignacio Avila.

Their Majesties, the King and Queen of Spain,
Don Juan Carlos I and Dona Sofia

Introductions to Descendants from the First Families were made, and a presentation of Jose and Marie Northrop's books, *Spanish-Mexican Families of Early California*, volumes I and II to them. Much of my family research was taken from these valuable publications.

After the daytime ceremonies was an evening gathering, by special invitation, at the Century City Hotel. I was given one of those special invitations and was on my way to meet the King. I was crossing the street at a signal-controlled crosswalk in the middle of the block when I got an unexpected two thousand-pound greeting. As I stepped off the curb, I only had time to notice a white hood of a car about to hit me. When I told my son Matthew the story, he said, "Why didn't you jump out of the way?" It was too late. I don't remember the actual hit but I do remember flying through the air for twenty feet and coming down on three points of my anatomy: my right hand, left foot and, right buttocks. Fortunately, I was holding onto that special invitation, which protected the palm of my hand. It left about a six-foot paper pulp trail as I skidded along the asphalt.

For a second or two, I lay there, but suddenly had the urge to jump up to see just where I had been hurt. A couple of ladies who had seen the whole thing ran over to me. I stood there and really didn't feel any immediate pain. The driver of the car came rushing up to me, telling me he was sorry. "Are you alright? I just didn't see you." It was about 4:30 in the afternoon, and the sun was low, shining directly into his windshield. It didn't help that he wore extremely thick glasses. By now I was leaning against a wall feeling a little weak, but not too bad. The witnesses, the driver and I exchanged information and waited for the arrival of an ambulance. One of the witnesses had made an emergency call. We waited and waited. Ten minutes had gone by. Two uniformed officers were passing by, and we asked them for help. They said they were off duty and to call the station…they just walked away. Maybe I shouldn't have gotten up. We waited another ten minutes, and still no ambulance and no police. We decided to go our separate ways since I said I was feeling sort of okay.

I made another attempt to cross the street. I was bound and determined not to miss the special invitation to meet the King and Queen of Spain. With each step the pain got worse. By the time I got to presentation hall I was hurting badly. Just then, I met my genealogist, Marie Northrop, who was chair-bound and always had a few extra canes with her. I told her what had happened and she insisted that I take one of her canes. I waited with all the other special people with their special invitations. The pain was getting unbearable. After about forty-five minutes, it was finally show time. The King spoke and every one listened. I listened too, but I couldn't understand a word he was saying. He only spoke Spanish.

It was time to leave. I could barely walk; the pain was so bad. With each step, it felt like that car was hitting me all over again. I finally made it to my car. I thought about driving myself to the local hospital, wherever that was, but my mother had just suffered a stroke and was in the Glendale Adventist Hospital. I had visited her earlier that day and, after my royal visit, had planned to go back that night. Also, my entire family was with her at the hospital, which was thirty miles away.

There was no one around to rescue me. I decided to drive myself to the hospital. When I finally got there, after driving at record slow speeds in my standard shift VW, I drove right into where the ambulances park and hobbled to the emergency and told the nurse I needed to call a patient's room before I was admitted. Thank goodness my cousin Donna answered the phone. I said, "When I tell you what I'm about to tell you, act calm and don't show any emotions, just excuse yourself and come down to emergency and rescue me." Of course, she handled it perfectly, but when she saw me she kinda flooded over with emotion. While having X-rays taken, I told her that I had never felt so much pain in all my life. I was a mess. It turns out that I had a broken hip. No other broken bones, just a lot of pain... everywhere.

I was living with Donna at the time. My wife Paula and I had recently separated, and Donna had offered her home as a refuge. The family finally got me back to Donna's, where they scooped me into bed and gave me a few painkillers. If only the King knew what I went through just to hear him speak Spanish.

I was sound asleep, knocked out by the pills when it hit; a good-sized earthquake. I don't know how, but there I was under the bedroom doorjamb in an instant, feeling no pain...until the shaking stopped. Whoa! Ha!...It felt like I had gotten hit all over again. Back to bed. Back to pain pills. Back to sleep. I was on crutches for a couple of months and then used a

Her Royal Highness
Infanta Cristina of Spain

126

cane for many weeks after that. I won the settlement for as much insurance as the driver had. It wasn't much, but it financed my eventual trip to Europe.

We had another Royal visitor come to our fair city, The Princess, Her Royal Highness Infanta Cristina of Spain. Originally, we were to receive her at the Avila Adobe, but the plans changed, either for security reasons or simply not enough room. The reception was moved to the Los Angeles City Hall Tower. The Tower is at the very top of City Hall. There are windows all around with a spectacular view of the city. Again, Mayor Bradley and the gang were there.

The Princess was just visiting the city. She probably had some official reason, but it didn't seem to be important to me at the time. She was very tall and extremely attractive. Maybe I was distracted. I did get a chance to meet her and shake her hand. Oh, by the way…she spoke perfect English.

Before the Future
EUROPE...AT LAST

Posing with the 'Little Mermaid Statue in Copenhagen, Denmark

I finally had the chance to go to Europe in 1989 after so many years of having seen it in the movies. I wanted to see that mysterious place that had been so important to me in my adolescent days. Europe is where my mind would go when I heard classical music or ethnic music from around the world.

I had been divorced for about two and a half years, and it was time. My opportunity came when I was discussing my plans with Per, my Danish friend from Art Center. He told me that it would be easier the first time in Europe to visit English-speaking countries in the northern part of the continent. He said he was going home to visit his brother and would be glad to show me around Denmark. I was to meet him one week after I arrived at the train station in Vajle, a town near where his brother lived. The plans were taking shape.

First I made flight arrangements. Next; a passport. Then I went to the South Coast Plaza Mall to the money exchange store to get Danish and Dutch money. I was on a high the whole time. I made a chart of the money exchange to make it easier for me when the time came that I wasn't in Kansas any more. I bought an inexpensive watch that could give me two time zones so I could keep track of U.S. time when I was across the world in another time and place. I bought travelers checks for the first time and a money belt to hide them. Next was a small automatic 35mm camera with a zoom lens. I also had my video camera with plenty of tapes. I wanted to capture my experiences for family members I knew would never get a chance to travel like this.

A friend from work gave me a few suggestions of things I shouldn't be without. One was duct tape. He said duct tape will fix anything temporarily and you never know what will go wrong.

Because I was going towards the beginning of winter, he said I'd better have a leather jacket. He said a leather jacket was particularly good when traveling because you could always bunch it up and stuff it in your duffel bag if you didn't need it. I said, "Won't it get wrinkled?" He said "Have you ever seen a wrinkled cow?"

Another item I took, which proved to be invaluable, was my new invention I called Fuzzy Belts. It was Velcro back to back with the loop on one side and the hook on the other. It became an extremely handy tool for quickly strapping loose items onto my travel bag, like my wrinkle free jacket, and small items I bought at the last minute, such as souvenirs and gifts.

My long time best buddy, Bill, took me to the Disneyland Hotel, where I met the airport bus to take me to LAX…and I was off! Scandinavian Airlines, of course. The flight was smooth and pretty

A stature of Hans Christian Anderson looking towards
Tivoli Gardens where Walt Disney got his inspiration for Disneyland

much uneventful. When we landed, it still hadn't hit me that I was actually in another country. The airport seemed like all other airports. When boarding a transport bus to my hotel, it finally hit me. The bus driver asked for forty-five krona to board the bus. Ah...krona...O.K. For some reason, I sorta panicked. Not in the true sense of panic, I simply froze for a moment. Time just stood still. I handed the driver some paper money and he gave me change. That was easy.

The first thing I noticed when I looked out of the bus window was that I didn't recognize any of the cars. A guy notices these things. There were no Buicks or Fords, of course, but I didn't even see any foreign cars I knew. I was definitely not in the U.S. It was really odd. The next thing I noticed was that the street signs were mounted on the corners of the buildings, not on poles like in most American cities. Being a graphic designer I seem to hone in on this difference. Big rig trucks had three sets of double wheels on the trailer instead of two. Most noticeably, everything was old. Actually, I expected that. As we traveled through the streets of Copenhagen, passing statues and old ornate brick buildings, it started to look familiar as in so many of the movies I'd seen over the years.

We pulled up to the train station, and I saw this grand old building with its old world history. It was magnificent. The train station was right across the street from the famous Tivoli Gardens, the place where Walt Disney got his inspiration for Disneyland. Even though I was feeling more comfortable, I still felt a little lost. When I entered the train station, my mouth dropped open. It was huge. There was a free-span canopy over the entire building with small shops inside. Here is where one made hotel reservations, bought train tickets, made tour arrangements or bought food. Unfortunately, all of the signs on these shops were in Danish. I just stood there wondering what next?

Then like an angel floating down from the heavens, I heard a voice, "You look lost, can I help?" The angel turned out to be an American from Michigan traveling to Sweden to attend a wedding. She was pretty and had a comforting smile. As she spoke, it seemed like this is where the music should start…but reality struck and, there I was simply a lost tourist being rescued by a helpful traveler. She had made the trip a few times and knew her way around. She helped me and generally comforted me, giving me confidence and strength to move on with my adventure. She showed me how to use the telephones, which were completely different from those I was used to. She pointed me to the right shop to get my hotel room, then wished me well and disappeared into the crowd.

The hotel was about half a block from the train station. Thank God it wasn't any farther. I had never been so cold in all my life. It was November 10th, 1989. Winter was well under way which had made the flight more affordable. The room was small, but very clean. I had asked for a shower in my room but, until the next morning, hadn't noticed that there wasn't one. I was tired and thrown off by the time difference, so it was bedtime for this weary traveler.

The next morning, I awoke to a new day in the land of the Vikings. Since I didn't have a shower in my room, I decided to use the community shower down the hall. By the time I got there I found the place had been well used. It was very wet and there wasn't any place to put my clothes. At least it was clean and the shower felt good. I had my first taste of Danish water as it streamed down onto my face. When I returned to my room and into the bathroom to shave, I saw some knobs on the wall that looked just like the ones in the community shower. I pulled one of the knobs and was immediately doused with water. The bathroom was also a shower room! I had wondered why there was a curb at the entrance to the room. It was to keep the water in. Upon further inspection, I saw the curtain track and that the curtain had been tied back. It all came together at once. But I was still all wet.

After drowning, I went downstairs to gorge myself on the all-you-can-eat-buffet. It was terrific. It gave me the energy I needed for my first adventure in Copenhagen. First thing on my list was to visit Tivoli Gardens. Then, I started walking not knowing quite where I was going. I found myself on the Strolle, a walking street with rows of quaint shops on either side. There were people everywhere, all speaking Danish or something I couldn't understand. Many were tourists…they were easy to spot. Once in a while, I would pick up on English being spoken. Americans were there too. I found myself down by the wharf when I suddenly realized I was very hungry. I grabbed a hot dog from the local street vendor. Hot dog vendors seemed to be everywhere. These were no ordinary hot dogs. Some were long and red, some were like sausages, and some were dark brown and very thick. None of them looked like a Dodger Dog.

I wound along deserted streets until I came upon a view of a huge fountain at the end of a street about three blocks away. When I arrived, I found myself at what seemed to be a very significant place. The fountain was of a warrior in a chariot driving four large bulls. I kept walking along the wharf, seeing other monuments and statues. From memories of movies I had seen, I felt as though I was nearing that place where the famous Little Mermaid statue would be. Sure enough, there she was. I had stumbled on her quite by accident.

I did what every good tourist must do: I took a picture of myself with that Little Mermaid statue just to prove I made it to Copenhagen. Apparently she was the guardian of the bay and the symbol of Denmark.

I continued up the path to an army fort passing more statues along the way. The fort was in the middle of a large park. There was an army guard walking the grounds as well as people walking their dogs… and me, the American tourist. When I emerged from the park, I found myself completely lost. I knew which direction I should be heading, but that was it. I was off the beaten path which actually was nice. I wound my way along strange but interesting architecture and people going about their business. Without realizing it, I wound up walking down the old familiar Strolla and breathed a sigh of relief. On my way back to my room, I stopped for some authentic Danish pastry. The shop looked like something out of a cartoon. Cakes dripping with icing and pastries of all kinds lined up ready to be consumed by watering mouths.

It was about 3:30pm and already getting dark. It was also very cold. I had my wrinkle-proof jacket on, gloves, a scarf and long underwear. The cold just went right through me. My stocking cap was pulled down over my ears, but I could feel the wind plowing right through my head. My feet suddenly told me I had walked too far. They wouldn't let me take another step. I sat on a bench and watched as the people passed, hearing every kind of language one could imagine. Copenhagen, especially the Strolla, was a melting pot for many people from many countries. It was fascinating just listening and watching.

I wanted to see what the nightlife was like in Copenhagen, so I stopped at a place that was advertising dancing. A man was at the bottom of the stairs that led up to the club and he told me that the club didn't even get going until 11p.m. or so. I had planned to be fast asleep by then...oh, well. He asked for forty krona admission (about $6.00). I figured this might be my only chance to check out the nightlife, so I got a ticket and headed back to my room to rest.

Once there, I slowly began to thaw out. The radiator heaters worked very well. The bedding was different from any I had seen. There were no sheets or blankets, only one white comforter with a zip-up sheet on the outside. That one comforter was really all you needed. It kept you very warm, in fact too warm at times. The toilet bowl was shaped very different, the opening wasn't like ours in the States. It was flat, then dropped suddenly towards the back, very strange. I tried to watch some Danish T.V. which was O.K...who needs sound?

I then bundled up for the walk back to the club. I climbed the stairs toward the music. Here we go. Danish nightlife. There were plenty of people, but no dancing. I got a drink and waited. Then, as though a bell rang for recess, the dance floor was crowded. My feet began to dance, but they couldn't respond to what my eyes saw. All the dancers were girls. Girls dancing with girls. The guys just sat there. I wasn't going to be the first male on the floor, so much for Danish nightlife. I made it back to my room just before freezing and flopped on the bed and fell fast asleep.

The next morning, I went downstairs to have my second continental breakfast, again great. I called Pers' brother with whom I'd made arrangements to meet, but I was a day early on their schedule. Having more time, I decided to visit Tivoli Gardens and do some more roaming. Per suggested I go to Amsterdam to see the museums and the canals. I bought a ticket on a sleeper that didn't leave until 10 that evening, so I stowed my bags in a locker at the train station and I took a local streetcar into the community to see what it was like among the natives. It was very enlightening, I realized. People are people all over the world. The buildings and cars were different but the people simply spoke funny. I felt like I was right in the middle of a foreign movie with no sub-titles. I couldn't understand what they were saying, but their actions spoke to me.

135

One of many Amsterdam canals that run throughout the city

That evening I went to a new popular place in town called Scalla. Open only six months it was the place to be. It was much like one of our enclosed malls with shops and eateries. It was the only place in town where something was going on. Christmas was just around the corner, so everyone was watching the decorations being arranged in the central court. There were food choices from all over the world. I selected Chinese but I shouldn't have. It wasn't very good. Nothing like good ol' America for good Chinese food. A glass of wine helped to pass the time. I sat at a small table overlooking the main floor and again people-watched. A girl sitting next to me asked the time, and we struck up a conversation. She was a striking young lady with short red hair. I bought her a glass of wine and listened while she told me of her life plan to become a fashion designer. An hour and a half passed before she excused herself and wished me good luck in my adventure in her homeland. When she stood to leave, she rose to nearly six feet. I met two other girls who were nurses, also, killing time at this special place. We all talked until it was time for me to board my train to Amsterdam.

After deciphering the very complicated train schedule, I finally found my train. The sleeper was interesting. It was the same size as a non-sleeper but had fold-down beds three high on each side. It slept six but fortunately, there were only four of us. My traveling companions were a young couple from England and a Moroccan who lived in Norway, visiting his cousin in Amsterdam. The English couple were very good-looking in a foreign sort of way, more so in the way they were dressed than anything. She was probably the most beautiful girl I had ever seen. It turned out she was to be on the front cover of Bride Magazine. She owned and operated an aerobics studio in Nottingham, England. Poor thing had a cold and was sniffling and not feeling well for most of our trip. Through it all, she still looked sensational.

Her boyfriend looked like a rock star. He wore a long leather coat that flared from the waist, and tight jeans. His boots and long hair went well with his narrow face, giving him that Mick Jagger look. It turns out he owned a beauty salon in Nottingham, which explained his flamboyant appearance. He was a hair stylist. The Moroccan was also a hair stylist in Norway. I told them that my mother was in the same business with a shop of her own. A small world after all.

As the train passed through the northern part of Germany, we were required to show our passports to a German conductor. When he came to our compartment and opened the door, I got a cold chill down my back. He stood there very stiff in his tight-fitting black uniform and ordered us to hand over our passports. I flashed back to the many World War II movies I'd seen and couldn't help feeling like I was suddenly thrust back in time.

We did as we were told and looked at each other with the same uncomfortable feeling as he walked away. A short time later, the German conductor returned. He gave us our passports and proceeded to pass out plastic wine glasses to each of us. He then popped the cork of a Champagne bottle and poured. With that, he pulled a newspaper out from under his arm and held it up for us to read..."BERLIN WALL TUMBLES"...The year was 1989, November 11. We all shared joy and tears on that happy occasion.

We arrived in Amsterdam at 9:30am. The Moroccan was meeting family so we said our good-byes at the train station. Norm and Vicki, the English couple, and I went to breakfast together at this little out-of-the-way croissant shop they knew about. They shared with me some of their dreams of one day getting married. They seemed to be very much in love.

After our morning visit, we parted. I just sat there and watched them through the distorted old-world, multi-paned-diamond shaped window as they walked out into the cold morning air, arm in arm. They stopped to hold each other, shared a good morning kiss, then off they went. I watched until they were out of sight, relishing that feeling they were experiencing, wishing it was me with that special someone walking down that cobble-stoned street along the canals of Amsterdam.

I got a room then took an excursion on a tour boat down the canals. It was a good way to get to know the city fast. When the boat tour ended, I walked and walked and found myself in the infamous Red light district. A virtual shopping window for sex. To my surprise, I saw families with their children taking in the unusual sites. I did not partake in the offering of young ladies selling their wares in the windows. I didn't want to bring anything home other than what I brought with me. Before long, it was dark so I went to my room to rest and watch some TV before drifting off to sleep.

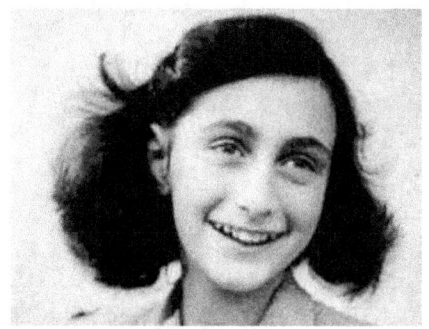
Anne Frank

The next day, I went down to still another great continental breakfast. I went on with my objective. Per had told me that I had to see the Rijks museum but to my dismay, it was Monday and all museums were closed. I continued wandering and stumbled on the Anne Frank House. I was very moved by the history and photos showing what she and her family had experienced. I went through the same secret door behind which she and her family hid from the German soldiers. I looked out the same window into the garden upon which she would gaze while wondering if she would ever be free again. My tears came, as did all others who were there…Very sad.

I continued on, but carefully. Apparently, cars had the right of way in this city. I found myself jumping out of the way several times. Bicycles were the main mode of transportation. Every imaginable type of person was on a bicycle, from old men to young girls in business suits on their way to work. A very interesting thing I noticed was special white bikes, set aside for community use. These bikes were all over town. One only had to ride to his or her destination and leave it there for someone else to pick up to use for their needs. The parking places for bicycles were amazing. It was a tapestry of wheels and frames; hundreds all jammed together along a rail or a fence.

I stopped to eat at a French café, the menu of which happened to be in French. I just pointed. It was delicious, whatever it was. Walking around, I found myself lost and found again. Eventually I made it back to my room where I collapsed in exhaustion. My train left for Vejle, Denmark, the next morning at 9. Once there, I would

Kings and Queens of Denmark laid to rest within the walls of Roskilde

meet Jorn, Per's brother, and we would go to the airport to pick up Per.

On the commuter train to the Amsterdam train station, I was sitting across from a Dutch fellow who was talking to another passenger. The Dutch language is very unusual to the ear. It sounds like a combination of Danish and German. Of course I didn't understand a word, but out of this strange sounding language, I picked up on something that was very familiar. They were talking about the Boris Gutinoff Opera. I suddenly said, "I know the Boris Gutinoff Opera." It turns out that I was sitting among a group of professional choral singers on their way to perform the opera. I told them that I had performed it while in the Concert Choir in college. It was a nice connection we all enjoyed.

On my way to meet Jorn, I decided to go on a little excursion. I got off the train in a small town called Roskilde, about thirty miles outside of Copenhagen. This town was the site of a famous ship museum. When I arrived, the town was still asleep. I found a place to rent a bike and rode through the town in the chilled early morning. It was like a fairy book village with cobble-stoned streets. Shopkeepers were sweeping with what looked like homemade straw brooms. Before I got to the museum I came upon an old church that looked very significant. I had again stumbled onto a historic place. This church was the resting-place for all the kings and queens of Denmark. I entered through large double doors. When they closed behind me there was an eerie silence. As I began to slowly walk down the aisle, I heard the sound of an organ. It wasn't music, it was like two or three off key cords. The sound came and

Roskilde Church

went. Leaving silence again. I actually felt a chill down my spine. The Kings and Queens were welcoming me, I thought. I was alone. Or so I thought. There was no other living soul in the place, which made this experience even more surreal. The church was fascinating. The bodies of Monarchs were in the walls, in the floor, and the more important ones had their own special ornate vaults with their likeness forever formed in bronze. This continued as I walked through the church. Except for the occasional organ interlude, the place was dead silent.

I finally found the ship museum, which was down a winding narrow path that led to the sea. There were five ships on display. These ships had recently been discovered in the murky waters just off the shore near the opening to a near-by bay. Over five hundred years ago the ships had been purposely sunk blocking the opening to this bay to keep their enemies from the north from attacking. This museum was also very quiet. The silence added to the mystery of these magnificent ships. The warship was over sixty feet long with a bow that shot up to the sky with the grace of a beautiful bird. I was left with a very lasting impression of the people who manned these vessels...The Vikings

Viking war ship

On the road again. Or the rails, as it were. It's a good thing I had given myself plenty of time. I had gotten turned around. It seems the train I was on for over two and half hours was going in the opposite direction. I noticed this when we came to a stop that wasn't on my map. The gentleman I had been talking to asked me where I was going, and when I told him he said I should have switched trains about a half an hour ago. He told me to get off at the next stop with him and get on track 2 going the other way. I did, and while on the way to track 2, I asked a conductor which track to Vejle. He said, "Track 4". I waited at track 4, and a train came on track 3 right behind me…I asked the engineer if his train was going to Vejle and he said, "yes"…Well, it was his train so I figured he must know…he did, and I arrived one hour after Jorn was to have met me…fortunately, he found me and we were off to pick up Per. We got to the airport with five minutes to spare. When Per arrived and I told him my story, we all had a good laugh after Per translated. Jorn spoke very little English, and I, of course, only spoke English.

It was dark when we arrived at Jorn's home and I got a good impression of how a typical Danish family might live. They had a feast prepared, not unlike a Thanksgiving dinner. Instead of turkey they served venison with all the venison trimming. Now I had never eaten a deer before, but I was game. And so was the deer, gamey that is. I of course was grateful and very hungry. I began to tell of my adventures, which entertained all except for Jorn's son, Meds. He didn't speak any English at all. He was actually a little scared of me. He had never heard anything other than Danish in all his three and a half years on this earth. He and I got to know each other after dinner through a children's book of pictures with both Danish and English words. He taught me Danish, and I taught him English. Jorn's girlfriend, Getta, the mother of the child, had lived with Jorn for almost ten years, since she was seventeen, but they never married. She was a Danish beauty…milky complexion, deep blue eyes and rosy cheeks with long golden blond hair.

The next day Per and Jorn went off to a meeting. Getta, Meds and I went for a walk to the grocery store and then out to the edge of the forest. We walked along some train tracks that led to an old wooden building where the local townsfolk were restoring an antique locomotive. The trees of the forest were thick and covered with newly fallen snow. I don't remember ever seeing a sky so blue.

The cold made Gettas' cheeks even rosier, adding to her glow from within. She told me of how she longed to go to a larger city to study nursing. After her child was born, it seemed her dreams were interrupted with an obligation she couldn't ignore. This is where I learned that she and Jorn weren't married and that she was in great need of a change. She told me that something must be done, even if she had to give up her son. Getta had never seen much of the world, let alone Denmark. She said Jorn was very set in his ways and simply wanted the family life with no complications. It seemed as though Getta would never see the world. As I listened to her pour out her feelings to me, this beautiful young princess trapped in her tower, I couldn't help but think that she was trying to send a signal to Jorn. I couldn't interfere, but I did fantasize rescuing her and taking her away from her confinement to show her the world she longed to see... just a fantasy.

Getta and her son Mas

When I left, I gave her a hug and thanked her for her hospitality and wished her good luck...she knew what I meant. As I turned to walk away, I felt her touch my back as to say "Thank you. "

My last night in Copenhagen was a most memorable one. I was able to get in-touch with Pers' cousin, Ulla, who I had known from a visit she made to the States about fifteen years earlier. I remembered her as a beautiful, thin blond girl with an intriguing accent. I was looking forward to seeing her again but when she came through the door of my hotel lobby, I didn't see the same person. She still had the intriguing accent, but she was shorter than I remembered, her hair was now brown, and she added about forty pounds.

I got over the initial shock and greeted her with a hug as if we were old friends. At one time we might have felt a little something for each other, but many years had passed and we were simply making a connection. We decided to go to dinner to this out-of-the-way place she knew of just off the main drag of the Strolla. The entrance was a

144

step-down lower-level type with no lights or signs. It didn't look like a restaurant at all but once inside the atmosphere hit you like a tidal wave. The place was alive with happy noisy people. The ceiling was dark and quite low. As you entered, you felt like you should duck your head. I don't even think the place had a name, although I'm sure it was known to the locals. Speaking of locals. There was nobody but. There were no more than ten tables, and there happened to be one table at the very back with two seats available. We were invited to sit there and with our backs to the wall we had the perfect seats for the show.

It seemed we were among a kind of private party. There were maybe two other couples, not with this group, which occupied the rest of the café. We were there maybe five minutes, and one of the men stood up and started to speak to everyone in a very powerful, loud voice. Of course, it was Danish, but the manner in which he spoke, I couldn't help but join in the laughter. Ulla would translate when she had a chance. But she said it just wasn't the same.

This man was apparently talking about someone in the group, and all were howling at his innuendos. Then he broke into song. He started singing this wonderful ethnic song, which caused everyone to sway and sing along. When he reached the chorus, everyone in the café including Ulla knew the words and they just sang their hearts out. The gentleman leading the group turned and gestured to us and everyone else to sing and enjoy...it was wonderful. Ulla pointed out to me that the group was a society to preserve the music and spirit of the Scandinavian people before there was a split in the countries. She mentioned that many of the members were prominent Danish citizens like television personalities, the director of a famous museum, etc...

In my mind, Denmark stayed with me for many weeks after I returned to the States. I just couldn't shake that far away feeling...A memory I'll treasure always.

NEW FRIENDS...
HELP IS ON THE WAY

And I lost millions

It had been a year since the divorce, and my employer, Ralph Allen, was tired of seeing me without a companion. He introduced me to someone he knew was soon to be single. When I met Nancy, I was intrigued by her bright smile and laughing eyes. On our first date, I of course talked about myself a lot. My favorite topic those days was my ancestry. For some reason, when I started telling Nancy my story, she couldn't stop laughing. I had hit her with the most impressive parts, and I guess she found them to be almost unbelievable. The more I told her the more she couldn't control her laughter. Nancy has this infectious giggle that kept me going on and on. Needless to say, we hit it off.

I was so anxious to meet my new date that I had forgotten to play the lotto that day. Something I did without fail, using the same numbers every time. Well, it happened. While sitting at the bar waiting for our table, there they were on the TV right in front of us; every one of my numbers. I looked at Nancy and said, You owe me three million dollars. I've never stopped playing those numbers from then on.

Nancy Wilson

One of the most noticeable qualities she has is her honest concern for others. In this case, me. She wanted to know about me. She took the time to listen and ask questions. It was great. Nancy was a woman who fed my ego, was pretty to look at, and so much fun to be with. Nancy was the first female companion of my own age I had spent time with since before I was married. She gave me a new way of valuing myself. We both loved the movies and would go fairly often. She would call me at work during the day, an early show then go out for Chinese food. We never became intimate, but somehow it didn't seem to matter to me. We had developed a special friendship. A friendship that was eventually challenged by a choice Nancy had to make.

We had been seeing each other a little over a year, and one day Nancy told me I was confusing her. She had known someone else who shared her same roots back east and felt a connection to him, yet I was in the picture. She had to make a decision. I told her that I valued her friendship so much that I would rather remain at least a good friend. I told her I couldn't lose such an important person in my life. We've remained as close as we ever were through the years and shared our good times as well as the not-so-good times. Nancy always checks on me to say hello and to see if I've found that special lady.

She's concerned about my general well-being and happiness. She has helped me when I hit bottom, always reminding me of life's pitfalls and rewards. She's still there, listening and asking questions, and because of our closeness over the years, she can put the meaning of life back into my soul. I'll always be grateful for Nancy's friendship.

August 30, 1997: The loss of The People's Princes leaving The Ritz Carlton-Paris at 4p.m. California time. At this very time I was attending the wedding reception of a princess in her own right, my friend Nancy, at The Ritz Carlton in Laguna Niguel, California. No one had heard the terrible news at the reception. We were all expressing our happiness for our dear friend.

I hadn't seen Nancy for almost two years. We'd been in contact by phone but I hadn't seen her new look. Nancy had some reconstructive surgery, and her new look was stunning. She looked like the princess she was. The place she chose to celebrate her new happiness was indeed a place of royalty. The dinner tables were centered with huge candelabras reaching over four feet towards the ceiling. I counted five forks, three spoons, and two knives. There were enough glasses to fill a warehouse. I guess I was impressed. The sixteen-piece band wore black tuxedos and sounded sensational. Nancy saw to it that I sat at a table with friends of hers who loved to dance. I took full advantage of the situation and danced with everyone in my path.

Nancy's own two sons gave her away, and, during their speeches at the reception, there was laughter and tears. It was a very touching presentation. Needless to say, Tom, the proud groom, was beaming with satisfaction. Nancy deserves the happiness she has found in Tom. He has been her constant companion since that time, after having won her heart…Remember, I was the other man.

I met Lori and Russ Walvoord at the time I was going through my divorce. They saw my hurt and knew firsthand what I was going through. Their marriage was the second time around for both of them so they had a little insight as to what I was going through. They invited me into their lives with understanding and compassion. Russ and I became close friends through a common bond of humor. He can be a silly guy, and I can certainly relate to that.

Russ Walvord

Each of us tried to out-do the other with our own brand of humor.

We started playing tennis on a regular basis. It was so much fun when I won, but he would beat me just as often. We were about even in skill and stamina.

Russ organized a yearly camping outing and invited my kids and me. It was the first time Matthew and Emily met Russ's son, Justin. When we pulled up to the campsite Justin was the perfect host, introducing himself and making my children feel welcome. He was a little older than they were but the age difference didn't seem to matter. We went on this outing three years in a row and had a great time each year. Justin was an aspiring young actor at the time and was in several children's productions. We went to see him every chance we got. Emily seemed to love the shows, especially knowing the star, Justin. I can't help but think it might have inspired her to join in on stage when she reached high school.

Russ is another friend who keeps in touch with me, helping me with financial advice and common sense tactics. He's a straight-shooting hard-hitting son of a gun. He always tells me the cold hard facts and keeps reminding me to not take things so personally. I find myself very fortunate to have Russ as a friend and a confidant.

One day Russ asked me to come to his house and play trains. Little did I know, was is a model train enthusiast. When I got there, I was impressed with his layout, but I told him his miniature trees had to go. One of the first jobs I had when I got out of the army was as an architectural model builder. I learned how to make miniature trees and made a few for him. He about fell off his work stool when he saw the results. This was a time when I was out of work, and the next day I remembered something Russ had said. He mentioned that model railroading was the second leading hobby in the U.S. I figured I should take advantage of this forgotten talent and turn it into a profit maker.

I started selling my miniature trees at a national train show that came into the local area about four times a year. I had every kind of tree you could imagine, large and small. I didn't make a lot of

Adrienne Thorne

money, but I made some. And some was better than nothing at the time. During one of my shows, I was standing there minding my trees, and this woman came up to my table and started to look at my efforts. I took a second look and, to my surprise and amazement, there she was again... Adrienne, that girl I dumped way back in high school, because of that dream. When she looked up and saw me, her mouth dropped open. She seemed to be just as shocked as I was. She and her husband were vendors at the same show, selling videos of train trivia, and had a booth not too far from mine. They are both attorneys and at the time, were living in Orange County, where I lived. She brought over her niece and introduced me, and told her just who I was. We all had a big laugh and I promised to get in touch to give her some trees, but I never did. Again, I jilted her.

If ever there was a Betty Boop in real life, I have had the pleasure of meeting her first hand. She and I worked in the same building and would talk from time to time. One day, I asked her out. Well, little did I realize, but I was in for a thrill ride to the funny farm. Carol Vail had the look and the personality of the famous cartoon character. Wherever we would go she was on stage giving whoever

Carol Vail

came in contact with her a chuckle, if not a side-splitting laugh. She became my Funny Buddy. Carol is a child psychologist and an ex-teacher. She is also an accomplished portrait artist. Her drawings and paintings fill her walls. Needless to say this cartoon character come to life has very special talents.

With her occupation, there comes a very serious side. My Funny Buddy has helped me through the years professionally with real problems. She's helped me with my children, my divorce and my own self-image. Through it all, I'm always left with one more ray of sunshine, and always a smile on my face. We shared one very special time when we both got into costume one Halloween. I was the Phantom of the Opera, and she was my bride. We were a goolish hit at the company party.

Another new friend who came to my rescue when I was feeling sorry for myself was Roberta Martin. She was a carpet vendor visiting me at my workplace. I told her how much I liked to dance and had no one with whom to dance. She said, -I'll dance with you."

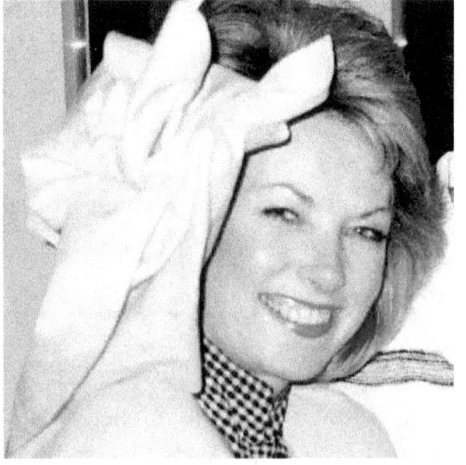
Roberta Martin

We agreed to meet at a dance place called The Hop in Huntington Beach. She brought two friends with her, and there I was with three ladies. The music started and we began our first dance. She called it the 'running dance'; I called it the 'choke'. It was the same dance. I hadn't danced like this since high school.

She wore a red dress and was looking good. We hit that dance floor with the pent-up energy of ten teenagers. They threw the spotlight on us as we spun and whirled around the dance floor. It felt like everyone was watching. When it was over the M.C. asked, over the loud speakers, "Where did they get that energy"? We both loved to dance and we were each pleasantly surprised at each of our abilities. Even on slow dances we were like Fred and Ginger. It was great. It was more than great. It was recapturing my youth.

Roberta is an exceptionally attractive woman. Wherever we went she got the attention. Of course, I looked good with her arm in mine. Whenever there was an occasion to include me on one of her company perks, I was there. We went out to lunch to the finest restaurants, The Magic Castle, Medieval Times and so many other places. Roberta included me on a four-day trip to Virginia to visit the carpet mill she represented along with several other designers.

The visit included a tour of Williamsburg, an historical colonial town preserved in the old traditions of early America. We stayed in an old historical hotel, believed to be haunted. Winter was just under way, and we had plenty of rain, which only added to the atmosphere. It was a very memorable visit to a place I might have never seen had it not been for Roberta.

Tennis anyone? Roberta played tennis like she danced. She even played Ping-Pong like she danced…very competitively. I could not keep up with her in any of the above accept dancing. She gave me one of her old tennis rackets that was ten times better than my old wooden racket. Watch out Russ. Roberta, like Russ, is very savvy. She has also been there to set me straight when I faltered. She tells it like it is and has caught me off guard many times. She seems to know how the world works and once in a while gives me a boost. I kinda wish we had some of those good times dancing again, but at least I do have the memories. We went skiing one time and she was down the slope almost before I skied ten feet.

I started going to a singles dance club where I met new people who have enriched my life. Carolyn Clark accidentally became my dance partner for the night when I was looking for another Carolyn. Her name tag said Carolyn, so I assumed I was addressing the right Carolyn, which turned out to be the wrong Carolyn who turned out to be the right Carolyn after all. She was the right Carolyn because I was enthralled with her zest for life. She is bright and witty and is very easy on the eye.

Carolyn Nelson Clark

What I didn't know at the time was that she was involved with another one of my passions, the theatre. She shared her season tickets with me and allowed me to indulge myself for the entire season. I enjoyed her command of the English language and her opinions on the educational system. Carolyn is an English Literature teacher.

We've shared the trials and tribulations of being parents of teenagers. On our first date, while waiting for her to come downstairs, she said, "Put on some music if you like." I chose from her selection of classical music, Vivaldi's 'Four Seasons.' I noticed a small pocket book on her coffee table. The title was 'Everything Men Know about Women.' I had to see what this was all about. Ready to learn insight to my intriguing date, I opened the book and found all the pages where blank! Looked like I was in for an evening of challenge.

Every one of our dates was filled with stimulating conversation on a variety of subjects. I felt a common respect that fueled a friendship unlike any other. She's a dichotomy of delights. On one hand, fun and crazy, on the other hand, dead serious and articulate. Our relationship came to an end after she said she was just too academic for me. She was right on. If only I could keep up.

Dick Eikmiere. One of the funniest men I know. And one of the saddest men I know. He, like me, has loved and lost. We're both lost in our fifties in the nineties. But we found each other. I don't know that finding each other is enough comfort for either of us but, at least we can cry on each other's shoulders once in a while. We met while selling time-shares at Dana Point. We were both there under false pretenses thinking we were being hired as tour guides.

Dick has the kind of personality that would do very well on stage. He has the charisma and sense of timing that brings him to the front of the line when it comes to entertainment. We, the salespeople, had to wait in a room for our next call to give our pitch. Dick was the entertainment. He kept everyone in stitches. He knew the jokes, he could ad-lib and, has an infectious giggle that kept us all laughing. I was, of course, one of his audience but when he was asked who makes him laugh he pointed to me. We saw the funny side of everything, including tragedy. Not until we left that job did we get to know the real tragedies in each of our lives. Dick is also an accomplished artist. A very sensitive talent going to waste. On one occasion, while waiting for a tour, Dick pointed to a badge he was wearing which read, "rub Dick for good luck."

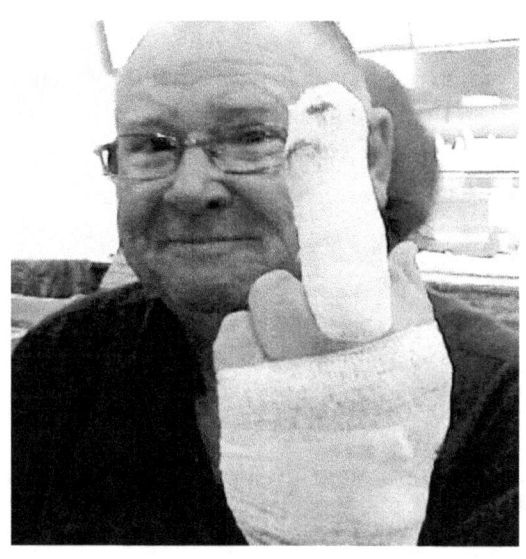

Dick Eikmire

We used to go to the singles dances where I met Carolyn. We did pretty well as a team, keeping the ladies entertained. Once in a while, he would get lucky; once in while I'd get lucky, but after a few dates we'd find ourselves back at the dance to try it again. It's tough out there. If a connection were made by one of us, we would be excited for the other. It's sad to see a funnyman down. The joy Dick has brought to so many should be appreciated. Vote for Dick and give him a good life. He deserves it.

While working with Dick I received a call from a former co-worker who offered me a job. There I was back in the design world working with someone I worked at my first job in the design business. The job was planning and design directing the opening of several outlet stores for a sports company known as B.U.M. Equipment. I was paid well and was in complete charge of the project which included stores spanning from the west coast to the east coast. My first project took me to the Big Apple. It had been thirty five years since I had been to New York, so this was an adventure I was ready for and getting paid to boot.

My first task was to fly into Philadelphia and rent a truck, pick up some fixtures from a store that had gone under and drive the fixtures to upstate New York for installation. This was all coordinated well in advance. It was left up to me to see to it that all went smoothly for the opening of the new outlet store. I designed new display counters as well as the check-out fixture. Carpeting, painting and graphics were all needed to come together to meet the opening day deadline.

NOTE:
I was asked to speak at Dick's funeral, saying I wish we could once again, help each other through life's journey. I choked up while trying to get the words out.

ESCAPE FROM NEW YORK

As the horizon began to lower she rose majestically in the distance like something out of a dream. I was on the New Jersey Turnpike heading towards Manhattan when the silhouette of the Statue of Liberty began to appear on the horizon. The road was angling down just enough, allowing her to slowly rise the closer I got. Then as suddenly as she appeared, she was gone. The road veered left, and she vanished behind the ever-familiar towering buildings of Manhattan. I was supposed to keep going north but I was so close... off the turnpike I went, heading right for that mass of concrete and millions of people.

I had forgotten my need to visit a bathroom, but I was soon reminded. Where does one pull over in Manhattan to use the facility?

Then it dawned on me. I was delivering fixtures to the new store I had designed and was driving a truck. I could park anywhere. I happened to find a loading zone right in front of the famous Sardis restaurant. I parked and rushed in, asking for the bathroom. "Are you dining here?" No, I'm just passing through but I gotta go! He begrudgingly

Sardis Restaurant
World famous for visits from Broadway personalities

replied, "I suppose you can use the facility upstairs. That section is closed." "Thanks"…there I sat in the famous Sardis restaurant, doing my business. I was honored. Sardis was famous because of the theater people who came to dine there after their performances on Broadway. Their autographed pictures adorned the walls of the restaurant, and anyone who was somebody was represented.

I figured I should walk around a little. After all, I wasn't too far from Times Square so off I went. The streets were lined with adult shops and everything looked dirty. Just as I was approaching Times Square, I was nearly knocked down by a guy who was racing down the sidewalk, crashing into anyone in his path. Right behind him were two healthy-looking individuals in hot pursuit. Who knows what the guy did but I'm sure he'll be sorry if these two brutes catch him. Continuing on, I finally made it to Times Square, where so many millions gather to say goodbye to the old year and hello to the new.

Darkness was quickly approaching and it was time to leave. I tried to blend in as a New Yorker, but I guess I stood out. An official greeter of the streets tried to hustle me, offering anything I desired. I desired to get to my truck safely. As night fell, these guys just came out of the shadows. I said no thanks and kept walking. This one guy stayed right with me, asking me over, and over "Hey you want some drugs? You want a date? I can get you anything." I walked faster, yet he still pursued. I darted across the middle of the block, hoping to shake him. As I was crossing in front of an alley I felt him only inches behind me. Instinct or memories of action movies took over. I don't quite know where it came from but in an instant I stuck out my leg and grabbed him by his shirt and threw him to the ground. He screamed, "What the hell you do dat fo?" I said, "don't you ever sneak up on me like that, you son of a bitch!" I quickly hailed a cab and was out of there. I told the cabbie what just happened, and he said I was lucky I didn't get stabbed.

I got to the sanctuary of my truck and tried to exit this unfriendly place. I found myself driving down narrow streets, through which I could barely fit the truck. Cars were parked on either side and, as I squeezed through, I actually hit one with my side mirror but I kept going down another street which looked like a main drag. I've never seen, or should I say, been swallowed up by potholes so big. I didn't dare slow down. I just wanted out. Finally, I came to the famed Holland Tunnel, which led to a tollgate leading out of the city.

It started to rain as I drove up to the gate. The sign read $3.00 toll fee. There were about six to eight toll booths with as many lanes all heading out of town. It seemed like everyone was queuing up for a

Theyer Hotel West Point Academy

race to escape from New York. I hadn't much experience with toll booths and certainly not the unmanned ones. The sign read $3.00, so I threw three one-dollar bills in the basket protruding out from the dark glassed booth. The gate didn't budge. It started raining harder. The racers behind me were getting impatient and began to honk. I got out of the car to retrieve my dollar bills, realizing that the basket only ate coins. Frantically, I searched my belongings for coins. Everyone I found I threw into the mouth of the hungry basket. The digital sign now read $2.51. I looked under the seat, in my luggage...$2.05, my pockets, the glove compartment...$1.98...honk honk...$1.56...honk honk honk. It was now raining so hard I could hardly see the basket. And then, as though the tollbooth felt mercy for me suddenly the gate slowly began to rise...I couldn't believe my eyes...at last, I'm free. Thank you, thank you.

When I arrived at my destination still wet and somewhat slackened by my harrowing escape, I was hoping for some kind words or a least. "How's your trip?" Nothing. All were busy stocking the store, and I suppose they were tired from the long day. We were near the famous military academy, West Point. Arrangements had been made for us to stay on campus in the Thayer Hotel, used exclusively for guests and families of the cadets. Again, another unexpected honor to experience such a famous place. We were to stay for about five days while preparing the opening of the new B.U.M. Equipment Outlet store in upper state New York. I was the designated store planner and designer. I had prepared plans, selected materials, and designed case goods. I was the overall coordinator of the operation.

Unfortunately, Easter fell right in the middle of our stay. The cool reception I got upon my arrival seemed to prevail. I guess I was considered an outsider, being newly hired to design and supervise the installation of a store they considered theirs. The staff I was to work with consisted of two local clerks, two merchandisers from our Los Angeles office, and their supervisor. They all met for breakfast the next morning at the hotel and didn't bother to invite me. When the Easter weekend came, they all went into Manhattan to see a Broadway show. Again, I knew nothing of their plans. So there I was, three thousand miles from home and surrounded by strangers.

Sunday morning, a special brunch was set up for visiting families of the cadets. It was a very lavish display of food and treats. I quickly found out it was invitation-only with name tags at every setting. Rather than sulk in my room, I decided to join in. As the salad plates were being passed out, I asked for one and simply helped myself to a feast of delicious food. I carried my plate piled high, outside to the picnic tables, where I devoured the tasty morsels and went back for more. Even though I was alone with hundreds of strangers the day wasn't a complete failure. When the staff returned from their little excursion, they said, "Gee, you shoulda joined us. We had such a great time." We all went to work Monday morning, keeping our distance.

I was to coordinate arrivals of fixtures, case work and all building materials…well, anything that could go wrong went wrong. I kept reminding the supervisor that they were asking for impossible deadlines. Two rolls of carpet arrived, and one was from a different dye lot…couldn't be used. They had to fly two new rolls from Los Angeles at great expense. The cabinets I designed arrived damaged…

they had to be repaired by a local carpenter. I'd say the only thing that went right was the white paint. Eventually, everything came together but I was blamed for all that went awry, and this was only the first of five stores. Fortunately, the others didn't have nearly the problems the first one had, but it sure set the tone for certain expectations. I was eventually let go because they said they were paying me too much and couldn't afford me any longer.

When I mentioned I had gotten a speeding ticket on my way to the airport, they said they couldn't do anything about that. The patrolman, who pulled me over, looked at my driver's license, noticing I was from California. "You know we don't drive fast here like you folks in California." I was ten miles over the speed limit and explained to the officer that I had to catch a plane. I was handed the ticket with no words spoken by the dutiful police officer. I missed my flight and had to wait several hours for the next transport to escape from New York.

Before the Future
MY MOTHER

I always wanted my mother to be in a rocking chair, knitting something, or in the kitchen making some home-made oatmeal cookies. But not my mother. She was a working mother. No time to be domestic. All of my friends' mothers did all the things I wished my mother could do.

The day I registered for school at Virgil Jr. High in 1953, the admissions officer thought my mother was my sister, or at least that's what he said. My mother was a very good-looking woman, and she sometimes caused men to act somewhat abnormal, in other words, like men.

I've heard the story of when a man ran into a lamppost while watching my mother walk down the street, which brings up something else about my mother I had trouble with during those awkward adolescent years. My ears would burn with some of the things she said. I'm sure if she knew it bothered me, she would have been more discreet.

Even while in high school, she would say things around my friends, that made me uncomfortable. I resented her and was embarrassed by her. Despite my feelings towards my mother then, she was very popular with all my friends, including their girlfriends. She always had a positive outlook. She made everyone feel special. Her energy and enthusiasm for life and all it had to offer were made evident when my younger friends would want to spend time with her. The girlfriends called her by her first name, Carrie, and actually thought of my mother as one of their good friends. Through my friends, I began to understand the value of who my mother really was: a kind and giving person simply enjoying life at every turn.

Every year, my mother would have an open house Christmas Eve party. She loved people, and having a party was her way of thanking everyone who contributed to her feel-good world.

My contribution was to bring the high school choir to sing Christmas carols at her party after visiting several hospitals in the area. From then on, all my friends in the choir and their girlfriends would show up year after year. As time went by, they would bring their wives, their mothers, then their children. Our family from San Diego, as well as any friend who didn't have someone to be with on that special evening, would be included.

There was always plenty of good things to eat and drink, but we weren't big on alcoholic beverages. Everyone pitched in and

164

brought their own special dish to share. One thing that I'm sure everyone remembers was the huge pile of presents under the tree. My mother and her sister, Aunt Dee Dee, would go overboard every year. When my aunt and my cousins arrived, everyone stopped what they were doing and formed a line to unload the seemingly endless array of new packages. There was always something for everyone.

My mother would decorate the tree and the house with a different theme each year. We all looked forward to seeing what new décor she came up with. She never had a traditional tree. The tree was always white with clear lights. One year the decorations would be all pink, another year all blue. Sometimes she would do a quick change at the last minute, but it was always spectacular. And with every New Year we would discover new angels added to her collection. My mother collected angels big time. Then one foggy Christmas eve, just like in the song, instead of Rudolph and a guiding light, our outside Christmas lights were a beacon for a family lost in the night mist. We invited them in, and they stayed for the entire evening, enjoying my mother's hospitality.

Every year, we would get a call from Fred Wilson, a choir member who had moved back east. We would all gather around the phone and take turns wishing him well. We would get surprise visits from Phil Brown, another choir member, and his family who had also moved away but managed to show up once in a while.

The Christmas Eve gathering was where we all came together to watch our lives unfold. With each new year came more surprises, a birth, a graduation, a marriage. Then, suddenly, the tradition came to an unexpected end. My mother suffered a stroke and was too ill to continue her yearly offering. The final Christmas party was held in her hospital room, ironically, one of the same hospitals where we all used to sing Christmas carols. It was sad to witness the end of a tradition that so many had looked forward to every year. The tradition moved to San Diego, where my mother had gone to be under the care of her sister. Of course, not all could attend, but we would get phone calls and cards from everyone wishing us well and remembering.

That final year before my mother went to live with her sister. Then, I lived with her and cared for her. After her stroke, she was unable to get along on her own. It was the first year of my divorce, and all fell into place so that I was there when she needed me.

If it wasn't for my cousin Donna, the Nightingale of the family, I couldn't have done it. She was always there helping me with the things I didn't have time for or just didn't understand. She knew what medications my mother needed, she took care of her banking and bills, and she did the laundry, and was there at a drop of a hat when I called her. Many times there were emergencies in the middle of the night. Again Donna was there. She never tired of answering my calls for help.

Cousin Donna Dee

Even though my mother couldn't do the things she used to do, she still was the same giving person every body loved. Spending time with her, I now saw my mother in a very different light. She was now somewhat helpless. I felt sorry for her. Sorry that she couldn't be the free spirit she used to be. Sorry for all the sorrow I'd caused her while I was growing up. Because of her stroke, she would slur her words or just couldn't get the word out, and she would actually laugh at herself. I would join in, laughing on the outside but feeling so bad for her on the inside. I became the son I should have been all along, giving her attention and helping her in any way I could to give her comfort. I tried to make her meals special each night. We would watch the TV. programs that she enjoyed. We would talk of old times, remembering together. I just wanted to try to give her all that was taken away from her.

After one year and many trips to the Emergency Room and the many healthcare givers that came and went, it was becoming evident that she needed more care than I could provide. I was away at work every day and didn't get home until after six o'clock. The healthcare giver would leave at five leaving her alone for sometimes over an hour.

It was decided that my mother would get better care living with her sister, my Aunt Dee Dee. Donna couldn't let her mother have all that responsibility. It was also a time that Donna had to make a decision. So Donna also moved to San Diego, back to her hometown, where she grew up. She was going home after moving to Los Angeles to live with my mother because her marriage that went bad. She brought her three-year-old son, David, and what belongings she could get away with. Donna found sanctuary in my mother's home. She eventually got out on her own, but my mother was her caregiver then, and now the tables were turned.

David, now grown, is in the position of caring for his mother, who had suffered a stroke in her later years. Tirelessly he gives back the loving attention he was given by his mother. David is now the caregiver for his mother. He manages a full time job plus running a videography business in order to keep up with the mounting expenses. Many

Cousin David

years ago David and I started this videography business funded by my old friend Mark Jason. Eventually, I dropped out, not being able to keep up with the physical demands. David has continued the business with resounding success. He has developed a following and is constantly in demand because of his attention to detail and passion for giving his customer the best that money can buy.

Mom and Cousin Rick out for a spin in a Miata

It was heartbreaking to pack up all my mother's belongings and move her out of the house she had known as home for over seventeen years. She didn't want to leave, but she knew she had to. We all said goodbye to that small house that was her 'independence'. She said goodbye to the city of her birth, and her home, where her doors were always open to friends and family...and strangers lost in the fog.

When my mother got settled into her sister's home, a new hero emerged: my cousin Rick. He was always giving my mother something to smile about. He made time for her, giving her a kind of special attention no one else could. He was the strong one who, with very little effort, could lift her onto her bed then tenderly give her a good night kiss. Rick was always called on to move, lift, carry, and generally be there for his mother and my mother. He never complained. He never tired of helping. I owe a lot to my cousin. He took my place when I couldn't be there. He made my mother feel loved and special and was always there to comfort her.

Of course, Aunt Dee Dee and Donna were doing their share of caring for my mother. Donna had found an apartment just across the street from her mother, so she was virtually there within seconds when help was needed. My aunt waited on her twin sister like no other could. She gave of her time and love so that my mother knew no discomfort. That connection between twins is very strong, and I knew my aunt was suffering with sorrow for her sister, much more than any of us could imagine.

I would visit my mother as often as I could, about every other weekend. The other weekends I would be visiting my children, Matthew and Emily in Palm Springs. After the divorce, Paula decided she could no longer handle the big four-bedroom home we owned, so she sold it and moved in with one of her sisters and her family. Every chance I got, I would bring my children to visit their grandmother. We always tried to do the celebrations around my mother like Thanksgiving, birthdays, Easter, and Christmas.

Occasionally, we would take my mother out for a ride to the beach or to Old Town or to the Warf. One time, we all went to the San Diego Zoo and had a great time communicating with walkie-talkies. We were always prepared, having my mother's insulin and orange juice handy at all times. We went out to dinner all the time. It was always Mother's choice. I would sit next to her and would help feed her. She liked dessert best and always wanted more. We all laughed a lot. My mother still had her sense of humor and usually surprised us with her wit and memory. One of the toughest things was getting her out of the car. She didn't have much movement in her legs and hardly any strength. Once we got her in the wheelchair we were on our way. We usually wore her out entertaining her.

After three, years my mother required even more care than Aunt Dee Dee could manage. It was time. Once again, Donna was giving of herself to help with my mother unselfishly and without complaint. Donna and I searched and searched for the right convalescent home. My aunt was fighting us all the way. She didn't want her sister to be put into a home. She couldn't make that decision. It was too painful.

The home we found wasn't prepared for the daily visits my mother received. Every day without fail, my aunt and Cousin Rick would visit my mother. Aunt Dee Dee would go there in the morning and stay all day. Rick visited two or three times a day when he could get away from work. My mother loved the attention. The nursing staff got to know my aunt and Rick on first name basis and would look forward to their return.

Rick still amazed us with his undying attention, he gave to my mother. He would take her for walks pushing her wheelchair to the nearest fast food place, and would sneak her some French fries or something sweet. One time he actually took her to a car dealer and took her for a ride in a white Miata convertible. The photo told the whole story: my mother's hair blowing in the wind and a smile from ear to ear. Once again, Rick, you're amazing.

When I would visit, it was so very sad seeing those lost souls sitting in their wheelchairs lining the way to my mother's room. My mother was very fortunate to have her daily visits. I again couldn't be there more than one weekend at a time. I almost felt like a stranger compared to Rick. He had brought so much life into my mother's existence, and I was only there for such brief moments. It's almost the way she was in and out of my life when I was a child living with my aunt and uncle, and she could only visit me once in a while.

My mother left us on March 19, 1994. All those who came to her Christmas Eve parties were there to say goodbye. Each in turn stood up and spoke of how Carrie, Aunt Tootsie, Mother, and Grandmama enriched their lives in just by knowing her as a friend, an aunt, a sister, a mother, and a grandmother.

Not far from our little ceremony, near Miramar Air Field, a coincidental fly-by of five F-14 Tomcats flew directly over us, as to say..."Goodbye, Toots, we Love You."

F-14 Tomcats on a training flight out of Miramar Air Force

Before the Future

MY COUSIN RICHARD RUSSELL HOAGLAND

The family lovingly called him Ricky. Ricky was our black sheep, so to speak. He was a rebel from the get-go. My earliest memory of his rebel-like ways was when as kids, we where dropped off at the Loma theater to watch serials and cartoons for hours while our parents went about doing what parents do when they don't have their kids to watch over. We filed into the theater and sat somewhere towards the front, my two cousins, Donna Dee, Ricky, and myself.

Once seated, Ricky got out of his seat and headed to the back of the theater.

Before the movie started, I got up to see where he went. As I walked up the aisle looking for my 6-year old cousin. I finally spotted him sitting with his arm around a young girl about his age. As the lights dimmed and as I got closer, to my surprise, my little cousin was actually making out with the girl. I didn't quite know what to make of this. I had never done such a thing, and I was more than twice his age. I hurried back to my seat and tried to make sense of what I had witnessed. I had nothing to draw on so I kinda forgot about it and went about watching the movie.

That was my earliest recollection of how advanced Ricky was in the girl department. From then on, Ricky always seemed to have a girl with him. Eventually, he had a more steady girl whom he would bring to the family gatherings. Anne was 14 years of age at the time, and I'm guessing Ricky was at least four or five years older. The two of them moved into the upstairs bedroom of my aunt's home. Rick, as we now called him, had his steady girl, but would do more than his share of entertaining other girls. It wasn't just girls he flirted with; he also flirted with the law. Getting into trouble just seemed to be a way of life for him. If it wasn't an unpaid ticket or two, or a drug bust or just being unruly, the San Diego police were always on his case. They knew Rick and would sometime wait just down the street hoping to catch him for some minor infraction so they could haul him in.

He caused his mother so much anguish and pain. She bailed him out of jail more times than I could count. There was a time when he was incarcerated at Campo, a low-security facility just north of San Diego, for possession. I remember visiting him with the family. He was very matter-of-fact about the whole thing and kept saying that he was innocent and that the police just had it in for him. It's true the police didn't like Rick and they might have pushed a little too much, but Rick probably deserved some kind of punishment.

As Rick grew older, he continued to be in and out of trouble for one thing or another. He had a string of ladies with whom he was always in touch, but through it all, Anne was true blue and stuck by her man.

Rick was very giving towards his mother, even though he had caused her many worried nights through the years. At birthdays, he was extremely generous with both his mother and my mother. Aunt Dee had a cesarean giving birth to Rick on the same day as she and her twin, my mother, were born. We would celebrate all three birthdays each year to witness Ricks capacity for love of his mother and my mother. He had a big heart, and when it showed, there was no other that could match his compassion. The downside was, it didn't last. The next day or soon after Rick was back to his unpredictable self. Again, Anne was always by his side. Never faltering when Rick would screw up.

Rick always tried to involve the family in the latest activity, such as having us go on "Family Feud." That didn't happen, but he managed to arrange for all of the men in the family to go on a white water rafting expedition. When it came time to choose teams to man the four-man rafts, out of five teams, not one asked Rick to join their team. Rick was just being himself and alienating everyone with his belligerent attitude. Rick wound up riding the raft, holding our camping gear all by himself. It was quite a site to see him on top of all the gear holding on to a rope as though he was riding a bucking bronco. He just didn't fit in. That was Rick, but we loved him.

Jumping ahead to when my mother was being cared for by her sister, and while Rick and Anne were still living in the same house, Rick was the strong arm of the family. When it was bedtime for my mother, Rick would pick my mother up and carry her to her bedroom and gently lower my mother onto the bed.

Eventually, Rick and Anne moved from his mother's home and had a place of their own. Anne had a steady job and provided a comfortable setting for them both. Rick began doing odd jobs, which developed into a small business. He even had business cards printed, painter, hauler, light construction, and so on.

Rick was now in his early sixties and settling down a bit, but still had a healthy enthusiasm for the rebel inside him. Anne had fronted the cost of a truck for Rick, which helped him with his business. It was bright red and unfortunately, easily spotted by the cops, who were always keeping an eye out for any infraction they could pin on Rick.

One rainy evening, while Rick and Anne were in the kitchen fixing dinner, they heard a noise coming from the side of the house. When Rick went to investigate, he found his truck being pushed down the driveway. By the time Rick got to the door, the one doing the pushing had jumped into the cab and started to drive away. Rick ran to catch the thief and found himself jumping into the bed of the truck. He started pounding on the roof of the cab, trying desperately to get the guy to stop. As Rick was yelling and pounding, he was hanging on for dear life. The driver started swerving back and fourth to try and shake Rick from the truck. Back and forth he went hitting nine parked cars as he went down the slick street. All the while, Rick is still managing to ride out the wild thrashing as the truck hit car after car. Eventually the driver lost control and smashed head on into a tree. Rick went flying out of the truck and landed on his back. He had broken several bones and was pronounced dead at the scene. Rick left us as he came to us. A wild ride…to his death.

Rick loved the ocean and was an accomplished surfer and swimmer. His wishes upon his death were to have his ashes thrown out to sea. During one of Rick's little escapades with the law, he ran out onto a pier and jumped into the sea to avoid capture. He was not caught that evening. We took Rick to that pier and, as he requested, gave him back to the ocean he dearly loved. He's out there with Daddy somewhere.

❖

Before the Future
FINDING MY FATHER

My father, Ray Osuna with his three sons, me, Randy and Rex, and his eight grand children, Randy Jr., Anthony, Corina, Ronnie, Ramon, Ricky, Matthew and Emily

When my son Matthew was four, he asked..."Where's your Daddy?" He had been familiar with his mother's father and wondered where *my* father was. Years previously I had asked my mother about my father, and all she was able to offer was that she knew nothing of him or his family. As a matter of fact she once said that for all she knew, they were all dead. When my own son needed to know where my father was, I was inspired to seek him out and give an answer to us both.

While attending a family wedding, my Aunt Jo leaned over to me and said, "I think it's about time you meet your father." She proceeded to tell me that though she had promised my mother she would never tell me of my father, she felt I should know him before he dies! At the time, he was seventy-two and in poor health. Aunt Jo thought I was now old enough to be told what she knew about my father. She said that she has been seeing him at family gatherings for years. I told her that I had just recently started to look for him and had been checking telephone listings. She asked that I call her to get his phone number.

I had been checking all the numbers listed under his last name and sometimes there was one with no answer. When I called Aunt Jo and she told me my father's phone number, which happened to be the same as the unanswered number, I told her she was off the hook. I had actually stumbled upon the number myself and Aunt Jo didn't need to feel as though she had betrayed her sister's trust.

The next day, I asked Paula to take the kids on an outing. I had to have complete silence and be able to concentrate on this very important phone call. I dialed. "Hello, is this Raymond Osuna?" "Yes," "This is Ron Crosthwaite." Silence. "Then you must be my son." "Yes, I'm your son." More silence. "I was told you are in poor health by Aunt Jo." He proceeded to tell me details of his health. Then we begin to just talk. He had questions, and I had questions. It seemed we both had the gift for gab. We talked for over two hours. Meanwhile, Paula had come back and had forgotten her key, and rather than disturb me she actually crawled through a window. She kept the kids quiet while I continued talking to my long-lost father. He told me that he felt bad about not having to try and find me, but knew of my whereabouts through his brother Ralph who kept in touch with my mother.

He told me he didn't blame me if I never wanted to see him because of what he had done. He felt that my mother had such a strong hold on me that he, my father, was painted as the evil father. I told him "I understand that both you and my mother were young and you both made mistakes. I forgive you both." We agreed to meet for dinner.

He asked that I not pick him up at his home. "I'd rather you meet me on the corner." I was a little confused but agreed. When I pulled up to the curb, this little old man peered into the passenger side of my car window and said. "Well, am I what you expected?" "Actually... no." For some reason, I had been looking for someone who rather resembled my mother's father, TaTa Al. He didn't look anything like what I had expected. I said, "Yeah." I consider myself to be a very good driver, but I found myself all over the road. I was understandably nervous. We got to the restaurant and ordered. He seemed to like the same dish I liked, enchilada verde. The connection had started.

It so happened that while I was attending Art Center and living just off Western Avenue, I dined at a certain restaurant that was also frequented by my father. As a matter of fact, we were both there at the opening and could have unknowingly sat next to each other. At the time, he also lived in that same neighborhood. He had married a second time and had two more sons. I had two brothers. Both boys attended Virgil Junior High School. I had gone to Virgil. When my mother remarried and brought me to Los Angeles, we lived in the same school district as my father. I used to take the 3rd Street streetcar to the end of the line, right across the street from Virgil Jr. High. I was only there for the first year until my mother and I moved to the north side of L.A., away from her second husband, the boxer.

We finished dinner, and my father decided that it was all alright for me to see where he lived. It was a rundown apartment building in a depressed area. I'm sure he was a little embarrassed about the surroundings. We eventually found a parking place among the broken down cars and made our way up to his place. As we climbed the stairs it reminded me of the old apartment I used to live in when I came back to L.A. The musty smell, the old carpet, the noisy children running up and down the halls. The place was indeed rundown, but it was home for my father. He had lived there since his divorce from his second wife, Barbara, the mother of my two half-brothers. He pulled out his keys and began to unlock the three locks to his door. It all felt somehow very familiar.

When he opened the door, to my surprise, there were open books everywhere. Artifacts were strung about as though they were being studied. Framed newspaper pages hung on the wall. It was not unlike a museum, or library or a laboratory. I didn't know what to make of it. He began to tell me stories; stories of our ancestry. It turns out that his father, my grandfather the one who had pursued us in the rain that fateful night, had done research on the family tree and history. My father was picking up where his father left off. I was fascinated. I started looking through the books, desperately trying to catch up. I asked questions and told my father that I too, was looking into the family history. This was a gold mine I hadn't expected. I was going to make the most of it.

I found my father to be a man with a slight chip on his shoulder, but I attributed it to his stature. He was a little over 5'3". He told me he had been in plenty of scraps as a kid and usually came out on top. He was as tough as they come. By the time I met him, he was an old man and with time had mellowed quite a bit. Randy, one of my half brothers, said I wouldn't have liked being raised by him. Apparently he had been very tough on he and his brother Rex.

As it turns out, when I named my son Matthew I unintentionally broke a family tradition. My grandfathers' name was Ramon. My father's name was Raymond. His two brothers, Ralph and Robert, had sons whose first names all began with the letter "R". My given name was Raymond Ronald. How was I to know?

I couldn't bring myself to call my father "Dad." He had developed a kind of isolationist attitude. He really had no use for people. He preferred monkeys. He actually had a family photo album with nothing but monkeys in it. He got the biggest kick out of monkeys of any kind. People, on the other hand, disappointed him, and he simply moved on to the other primates. He also wasn't very vocal regarding appreciation. When something was done for him he would just stare at you for a second as though he couldn't believe you had done something for *him*. He rarely offered a "thank you" but you could tell he was very grateful. He just couldn't express it.

We invited him to our family functions and tried to bring him back into the fold. You could tell he appreciated us including him. There was a hitch, however. My Aunt Dee Dee had never forgiven him for what he had done to her sister. She refused to accept him back into the family. For any family gathering he attended, Aunt Dee Dee wasn't there and vice-versa.

I sat my mother down and told her I had something important I needed to discuss with her. She looked at me and said, "You found your father." She then began to tear up. Somehow she just knew. We had a few awkward moments where my mother tried to explain why she hadn't mentioned my father to me, but it was done. This had happened so she accepted it.

The very first family gathering my father attended was my son Matthew's 4th birthday. My mother had to prepare herself for this meeting. She hadn't seen my father for almost forty years. I had never seen her look so good. It was obvious she was going to make an impression. When we saw my father pull up in front of the house my mother grabbed my one-year-old daughter Emily into her arms and hung on for dear life.

Out of the first car came my father and his girlfriend. Out of the second car came his second ex-wife and their third son, Rex, along with his wife with his three sons, Ronnie, Ricky, and Ramon. Out of the third car came my father's second son, Randy, with his wife and three kids, Randy, Anthony, and Corina. In all, there were thirteen in his entourage. None of us was ready for this. It was extremely awkward at first but in time we all remembered the reason we were there, to celebrate Matthew's birthday. He was finally to meet my father. The most memorable moment was when I looked out of the window to find my mother and father sitting under the 100' redwood tree talking…just the two of them. I wonder to this day what words were spoken after forty years. What thoughts were expressed? What emotions were felt?

I continued to include my father in our lives for over nine years until he finally died. He once told me that the two most important things that had happened to him were his present girlfriend and me coming back into his life. He particularly enjoyed his new grandkids, Matthew and Emily. He would invite us out for pizza and spaghetti. He was known as Grandpa Ray. I tried to see him about two or three times a month. We usually just went out to dinner, but it was always a time well spent. I got to know more and more about the mysterious father who hadn't been there while I was growing up.

He was in an auto accident, which damaged his knee, so when he tried to join the Army during WWII he was rejected. He served his country by joining the CCC's (Civilian Conservation Corps), where he became the cook and later the company clerk. He was always issuing himself passes and generally bucking the system anyway he possibly could. He was very resourceful and made good use of his position.

Childhood hadn't been an easy one for my father and his two brothers. Their mother died when they were quite young, and their father didn't remarry right away. They made their living by hauling rocks or hay or wood, just about anything they could load into their father's wagon. They lived a hard life on the road, sleeping in tents on the ground. They would also go from farm to farm, milking cows or performing general farmhand work, anything to keep food on the table. My father, Ray, did the cooking, for he and his brothers and became the designated range chef. By the time I caught up with him, he was pretty much eating out of cans. At seventy-two, he was still strong as an ox and kept in shape by working at his original

Grandpa Ray, my father, hard at work as a hat blocker at age 72

profession part-time. He went back to hat blocking, a long lost art that used to be done by hand but is now automated. He took the city bus to downtown L.A. every day and worked about twenty hours a week. When I went to visit his workplace to see just what hat blocking was all about, I found just how physical his job really was.

This place was a real honest-to-goodness sweatshop, located at 7th and Broadway right in the heart of the city. My father wore a leather apron, a short-sleeved shirt, and was surrounded by hundreds of hat blocks dating back to the thirties. His workplace consisted of a large steam oven, a kind of ironing board, several strands of rope of varying lengths, and stacks and stacks of hat blanks. These blanks consisted of a flat felt-like material, round in shape, and came in various colors. His task was to take a blank and iron it over a given hat block, and then tie a length of rope around the rim then pull it with all his might. Next he would iron the blank with a hand iron to make it form snuggly around the block and put the form into the steam oven.

183

He did this over and over again with amazing agility, never seeming to come up for air. He was positioned at the head of two rows of ladies putting the finishing adornments of ribbons and feathers of all colors and sizes.

He proudly introduced me as his first son. In those days, I was all decked out in a suit and tie, working in a downtown architectural firm…uniform of the day. I was the professional son he never knew about. Now it was time to show me off, and he did. We would stop along the way to our lunch, where he would introduce me to various vendors. The man at the newspaper stand, the barber he frequented, and a shop owner or two.

His favorite place to go to lunch was the Bonaventure Hotel. We would meet at his workplace and walk through the crowds to the grand glass building he loved so much. He said that before I came back into his life, he would just sit in the lobby overlooking the fountain below, enjoying the view and the splendor of it all.

Bonaventure Hotel

My father loved the old Los Angeles. He collected books on the city, articles of its past, and the romance of its history. He would talk of how it used to be with its clean air and all the fancy clubs he would frequent. His passion in the old days was to hang out at piano bars and listen to live music. Drinking and smoking were what one did in that environment, so he did, until one day he looked in the mirror and said, "That's enough." With that, he quit cold turkey. After smoking and drinking all of his adult life he changed with one look.

Ironically he met his girlfriend, Dolores, while at one of these dives and found her to be the best thing for him. To his dismay, she

184

turned out to be an alcoholic. She saw something in him that made her straighten up to a point. Whatever the attraction, together they filled each other's time in their declining years. When he went into the hospital for a routine prostate procedure, he had a mild heart attack. As a result, when released from the hospital he became very weak and could no longer be on his own. He and Dolores came to the agreement to go their separate way. He knew he couldn't keep up the life style they had shared over nine years and rather than burden her, he wished her well and thanked her for the many good times they shared.

Ray wound up being cared for by his second wife, Barbara, until his death. I would still take the kids to visit him, and we would go out from time to time. One thing I did for my father in his final years was introduce him to the world of the VCR. He loved the old movies, and this was a way he could buy and rent all of his favorites. He had accumulated quite a collection in those few years. He confessed to me that he had a serious crush on Ginger Rogers. Of course, there were plenty of the dancing couple in his collection. I took him to see "Dances with Wolves" and he said it was the best movie he had ever seen. To this day, when it comes on TV, it reminds me of my father.

On his deathbed my father said, "I wonder what it's like on the other side?" Soon before he passed I looked into his eyes and told him I loved him…then he was gone. I knew him for a total of thirteen years, my first four and his last nine.

Before the Future
EARLY MARRIED YEARS
Another Beginning

I met my wife, Paula, while designing a medical facility with a classmate from college, Tony P. We were in the process of gathering information on various doctors to incorporate them into the Cotton

Monterey The original capital of California

Medical Center. Dr. Cotton had brought several offices together to form a limited partnership. Dr. Cotton's son, Hollis, was working with us and knew most of the Doctors personally. He mentioned to me that a certain office had several single women working there and that I should check out one in particular.

When I came to the office to measure their space, I noticed Paula to be a nice looking and not too pretentious young lady. I was thirty-five and had never married. I dated as often as I could, not wanting a weekend to pass without company. The women or girls I chose to date didn't always have that bring-home-to-meet-the-family look. My experiences with women were hit and miss, mostly miss. By now, I had been in love four times and lost in all four cases. My quest now was just to have a good time with no immediate plans for the future. But time started to catch-up with me. Thirty-five and never married. People began to talk. "What's the matter with him? Is he gay?" etc.

I believe I was waiting for that special feeling to come around again. I wanted to be in love. I wanted to love. I also didn't want to be hurt anymore. When I met Paula, I was not dating anyone in particular and had the weekend open. I asked her out for that weekend, and she refused, saying it was too soon after meeting me. She knew how to play the game. She agreed to see me the following weekend.

I rang the bell, and one of her sisters answered the door. A tall, good-looking blond greeted me and asked me in to wait. I was very impressed by her, appearance and then another sister came into the room, I guess to check me out, another knockout. Then her third sister appeared. Only fourteen, she also had great potential. These three sisters were the type I would always try to date, but never had much luck. Paula then appeared with her wholesome and comfortable look, much more plain than her younger sisters, but somehow more real, more approachable. Down deep I was looking for Paula more so than the surface of her sisters.

Hidden Valley Grove Yosemite National Park

Our first date was an awakening for me. Paula was indeed more of what I wanted and needed. She complimented me on my

Madona Inn, San Louis Obispo, California

driving. That may not seem like much, but I considered myself to be an

exceptional driver, and she picked up on this. We had a great time that first date. Mexican dinner and the movie "Young Frankenstein" created a fun atmosphere for our beginning. Paula was too good to let go. I chose not to date any others. We saw each other every weekend. Paula made me laugh. She appreciated my dry sense of humor. We sang while waiting four hours for the opening of Star Wars. She knows the words to every song ever written and I knew the melody. Together the songs rang true and brought us closer together. We danced to the Glen Miller band at the Hollywood Palladium. We did a lot of special things together.

Paula's parents were as different as night and day. Her father commanded a lot of respect. He was a self-made-man relying on no others. He had his studio in the basement where he practiced photography. He was a photographer in the Navy and followed his training into professional life. He was very good at what he did and as a result, made a very good living. He wasn't much for sharing, especially with his family.

When he bought the house Paula was living in when I met her, he negotiated to buy all of the old furniture with the house. The carpet was very worn, but he didn't replace it. The place needed painting desperately. He chose to buy another gun to add to his collection instead. The four sisters had no curtains on their windows. He never made an attempt to give them the privacy they so disparately needed. When I came over he would bring out his latest purchase. He called them investments; a Remington sculpture, an antique gun, a silver belt buckle, a painting; anything to fill his curio cabinet, but nothing to improve the living conditions for his family. He bought himself a new Mercedes and drove it exclusively. Paula's mother drove an old Rambler. The car was drafty and dirty and wasn't very reliable. One day when we were washing the Rambler, we actually found mushrooms growing on the floorboard of the back seat. Gifts to his wife by the miser amounted to one gadget after another to either service the kitchen or clean the house; never anything of a personal nature. He punished the girls very harshly driving their self-

Mel and Jan Schockner sharing their home with us on our honeymoon 191

confidence out of existence: all four were affected by his overpowering dominance.

I got along famously with Paula's mother. Mary was a delightful conversationalist. She and I would talk and talk about just about anything. She had a great sense of humor and little sayings that would always put a smile on your face. While helping her third daughter change her son's diaper, having all girls, she exclaimed, "That's a handy thing to have on a picnic." In her day, Mary was quite a looker. By the time I met her, she had been stricken with crippling arthritis and was in constant pain. Her hands were so deformed that she could hardly grip anything with any dexterity. Her walk was very slow, and with every step, she suffered great discomfort. With all her daily suffering, she was always a joy to be around, never complaining, never asking for help. She went about her chores as though nothing was any different. She was a great cook and rarely needed help in the kitchen, although her daughters were always there, especially Paula. Paula learned the art of cooking from her mother, and I was the direct beneficiary.

There was a time when Mary had enough from her selfish husband. She managed to drive to our house, and ask that we help find her an apartment, so she could have her freedom. It never happened. She went back. Back to the abuse. Back to the old furniture. Back to the mushrooms.

When Mary died, it devastated her daughters. Thank goodness all were married and out from under their father's thumb. Paula was the closest to her mother, and suffered a long and trying loss. Not until many years after our divorce did Paula finally deal with her anger towards her mother; angry her mother didn't do more to protect her daughters from the ugly dominance of their father. Paula has now found peace in the Word and is able to cope with her bottled-up feelings.

Paula and I had been raised with the catholic faith, and chose to marry in a traditional Spanish-style church in Pasadena, St.

Stopped for a snack by a river,
Deer outside our window at our presidential suite
The interior of Mel and Jan's retreat and studio

Elizabeth. Her oldest sister was her maid of honor, and her other two sisters and one cousin were the bridesmaids. I chose my old buddy Bill
to be my best man. George and Pat, my old high school friends, along with Cousin Rick, were my ushers. I wanted to include Mark in the wedding, but we ran out of bridesmaids and I wasn't going to not include my cousin. I was best man at all my friends' weddings as well as a Huppah Holder at Mark's wedding, and I held his son, Willie, at his bris. Cousin Rick has never gotten married and probably never will.

In order to marry in a Catholic Church, we both had to produce our baptismal certificates. I was baptized Raymond Ronald Osuna, but had been using the name, Ronald Raymond Crosthwaite for the past twenty-seven years. I then had to legally change my name so the wedding documents were in my current name.

Mirror Lake, Yosemite National Park Our view from our President's Suite

Needless to say, when we announced wedding plans to my mother over a Chinese dinner, she couldn't finish her meal. She waited a long time for her only son to get married. Paula's mother asked me if I was flattered that someone so much younger than I agreed to marry me. I hadn't really thought of the thirteen-year age difference, all I that knew was Paula would be good for me. I needed to settle down. Paula was good. She was very domesticated, having been the predominant caretaker in her family, helping her ailing mother and younger sisters. She could cook, she would be loyal and she was spiritually strong. I must confess that I wasn't in love with her, but I *did* love her, and would grow to love her more. She later told me she actually felt the same. She and I agreed that we were still carrying a torch for our first love.

Our wedding was a beautiful ceremony. Our reception was the best party we could have thrown for our friends and families. We were having so much fun, I never even got to taste the wedding cake, and I had picked it out; Rum cake with custard filling....Yum! I heard it was delicious. The music and dancing were going along without a hitch. The food was outstanding. Then, to our surprise, the Studio Gang provided a gift for us all. Their wives had all been taking Polynesian dancing, and they brought their music and their troop in full costume to perform. All my old uncles' eyes were fixed on the dancers' gyrating hips. The girls put on quite a show doing both Hawaiian and Tahitian dances. Pers' wife Becky ended the presentation with "The Hawaiian Wedding Song," directing her performance to Paula and me. It was an unexpected treat that really topped off our party for all in attendance.

My new bride and I moved into our little white cottage apartment on Huntington Drive in South Pasadena. It was perfect. There was an ornate fireplace, a picture window overlooking the court, and a screen porch, two bedrooms, and even a small formal dining room. The kitchen had a box window where we later hung our birdcage. Our firstborn (hatched), a little finch, was our first hatchling. The real mother and father were Sugar and Spice. We named the mother Sugar because she was white and pure. We named the father Spice because he was full of it. He just couldn't wait for his little guy to grow up, and he was at it again. Before you knew it more eggs were laid and the first little bird was kicked out of the nest. We had to hand-feed that little finch until he could fend for himself.

He turned out to be quite a tame bird, for a finch. We could put our hands right into the cage and he would land on our finger waiting for a treat.

We had taken that great step and now needed to begin married life. We started with our honeymoon

Paula wanted to go to Hawaii but I thought it would be too expensive so I suggested traveling up the coast and see California. She finally agreed, so the plans began to take shape. First stop, the famous Madonna Inn. As we approached the off- ramp to the hotel we found ourselves in a parade of newlyweds. It seemed everyone with their right blinker on was finding their way to the infamous hotel.

We reserved the Green Room, green being Paula's favorite color. Everything was green: the bed covers, the sheets, the lamps, the rug, the furniture, the chandelier, the walls, the ceiling, even the toilet bowl. When we finally emerged from our greenness, we immediately ran into other couples who wanted to share their redness or their blueness. We all had a great laugh over the whole ridiculous environment. Oh, did I forget to mention the men's bathroom at the adjoining gas station? You walk up to this magnificent mural of a vast mountain scene with a stream running through the room. Well, sir, you stepped right up to that stream and that's where you did your business, right there where nature intended you to go. And they say the corn is in Kansas.

Our next stop was in Monterey, the original capital of California. We stayed in Monterey, but became typical tourists in Carmel. Cheaper rooms. We drove the Sixteen Mile Drive and walked the perfect streets of the Jewel City, enjoying the perfect weather. On to San Francisco where we did the wharf thing, the trolley car thing, the up and down the hills thing, all in all having a wonderful time exploring this magical city.

We actually stayed across the bay in Tiburon, a quaint little city overlooking the San Francisco Bay and the famous Alcatraz. Traveling across the Golden Gate Bridge is an unbelievable experience. It seems to go on forever as you're taken up into the clouds and over the ocean with its miles of cable and brightly orange painted steel.

On one of our off days, I decided to take a little trip up the coast to show Paula a stand of redwood trees that Per and I had photographed while shooting, for the very building Paula was to work in, before I met her. Our destination was called Hidden Valley Grove. I didn't remember just how hidden it was. Four hours later, we were there. It was the kind of place you imagine in fairy tales of enchanted forests in another time. Tall majestic trees reaching to the sky with sharp rays of sunshine bursting through the folds of the canopy above. The entire ground was covered with huge lacy, ferns that danced in the gentle breeze. There was a stillness that kept you from thinking about anything in the outside world. It was indeed the work of God. Obviously, a place one had to share with his new bride.

My college buddy Mel Schockner and his bride of eight years, Jan Rosetta, came to this northern part of California to build their dream home. And a dream home they had. Nestled in the forest of Mill Valley just north of the City, it was a kind of artist community. They invited us to stay a couple of days with them in their dream nest while we were in the area. Their home was a simple square that consisted of a large open space with skylights, open beams, and hanging plants everywhere. Mel and Jan are both artists and utilized the space for both studio and living space. The divisions were simply marked by the functional furniture of the area. The kitchen doglegged around to the right, allowing a wall for the privacy of the only bedroom and bathroom. The sides of the house were all glass, reminding you of just where you were. A balcony jutted out into the trees from all sides allowing you to visit this wonder, and smell the freshness and experience the quiet. We had a very special time there sharing, with our good friends this place of peace.

The final leg of our tour of the state was a stay in Yosemite. When we arrived on our day of reservation and requested our room we were led to a very rustic cottage-style bungalow. When the door opened, the first thing we noticed that was there were only two single beds. Two single beds? We were on our Honeymoon! Back to the front desk we went with a good excuse not to accept the room. To our surprise, the place was extremely busy. Little did we realize we had arrived on Columbus Day, a three-day weekend.

When we told of our situation the nearby crowd of tourists gasped and a small commotion started to ensue. The clerk called the manager and the manager made a few calls then profusely apologized then proceeded to take us himself to the President's Suite. It was the best room they had. It had a view of Mirror Lake with a stream running by the window. It was pretty cool. By the way, there were two queen-sized beds. More than we needed, sorta.

The next day we explored the meadows and the valleys and the mountains. We even saw a family of deer right outside our suite window. Yosemite is another of nature's wonders. You can't leave without a profound feeling of humbleness. A perfect ending to our excursion was when we stopped along a river to have a picnic lunch and enjoy that last breath of fresh air before heading back to reality.

As our life together started to unfold we, began to think about our future regarding raising a family. Paula questioned if we should have children, and I came back right away with, "If anyone should have children, it should be us." Our reference was regarding her sisters, who started to think of the same thing. Like I mentioned earlier, Paula's sisters were a little on the wild side. They weren't bad, but they were girls who liked to have a good time and sometimes showed poor judgment. Paula and I, on the other hand, thought we were more mature and responsible, so if anyone should be raising a family, it should be us.

Now it was time to find a more permanent home. We started looking. What lead us to the house in South Pasadena was it's school system. One of the best in Southern California. Paula's parents helped us with the down payment and there we were in our own home in a great neighborhood.

We painted, hung wallpaper, and bought furniture for our new little nest. There was a coastal redwood tree in our front yard that stood almost 100 feet tall, and a fairly large grass-covered front yard. The two-car garage was in poor shape but it was perfect for storage and a kind of workplace for me. The backyard was very small and wasn't much to look at, but eventually we created a play area for our two children when they came along. There was also a partial basement where I could get away and do graphic projects when the time was needed.

While hanging wallpaper in the kitchen, I discovered dry-rot at one outside corner. I had to repair it by going under the house and removing the bad wood, and replacing it. The stairs leading up to the kitchen back door also needed repair, so I built an entire new staircase. For Christmas, I asked for tools, and they came rolling in. They came in handy for all my house projects. Eventually, I designed and built a fence for our front yard, mainly to keep the dogs out and our children in.

We conceived our first child while vacationing in Hawaii at Paula's parents' time-share condo. When it came time to name our little guy, we gathered all our good friends at a restaurant and asked for their vote on the names we had been considering. By committee, they chose the name Matthew, and it stuck. Both Paula and I chose Matthews's middle name. We each had a favorite uncle named James. Matthew James was born on April 3rd at Huntington Memorial Hospital in Pasadena.

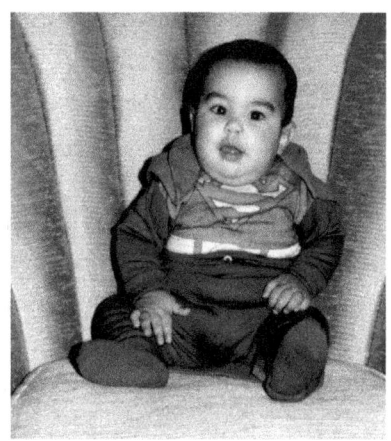

Matthew James at one year

Our son became the joy of our lives. He came out with a little more hair than the average monkey, so we immediately called him our little monkey. He was a good-natured little guy and was always smiling. We loved him so much. I loved him so much. A father couldn't be prouder. We painted the walls of his room a sky blue and I cut white puffy clouds out of white shelf paper and stuck them on the walls. I made a rainbow out of plywood and hung it over his crib against the wall. I built a large toy box that could be pulled out from under the crib for all the toys he started accumulating. My mother was thrilled to be a grandma and, of course, so was Paula's mom.

We were constantly reading to Matthew, trying to give him the best we could offer. As he grew a little and, began to talk, I would sit with him, asking him to name each toy I would pick from the toy box and in turn he would tell me the name in his cute little child way. He also like to, what he called, "wrestle and roll around" so we did a lot of that as well. On his first birthday. It was so much fun watching him discover sweets as he dove into his birthday cake.

Each year, Matthew rewarded us with his love. He was a sweet child with an undying curiosity. He was always there, right under my feet, wanting to do what I was doing, whether it was mowing the lawn or working on my car. He was all boy.

Matthew loved anything to do with sports, so like all good parents, we started job in soccer. Next came basketball, but that didn't take. One day we took him ice skating and when the public skating over, there were young boys practicing ice hockey. Matt needed to try, so after $450.00 work of equipment, he started ice hockey. At first he, like all the other boys, was awkward on the ice, but it didn't take him long to become pretty good. Nowadays, he can ice skate with the best of them.

About this time, Matthew entered middle school, and gave basketball a try. He did okay at basketball, but the sport that stuck was football. He went on to play in high school as well. He was on special teams, and did the long snap. I couldn't believe that Matt didn't mind putting on that football uniform in the heat of the desert. His practice games were grueling to watch. Thankfully the games were usually at might. One if the most memorable games for me, was his last game. There was light rain falling, and after the game, Matt came off the field slowly walking toward me with his helmet in his right hand and his left arm around his girlfriend. Noticing his sadness, I turned my video camera off. His head was down, and when he saw me he said, with tears in his eyes, "Dad, this is my last game." He loved playing football so much, but he knew he wouldn't be playing any longer.

Matthew has made me so proud to be a dad. He has excelled in so many things. I introduced him to the "MacGyver" way of solving problems and he's taken it to heart. He is very capable of thinking on his feet. Something else I love about my son, is that he has a heart of gold. He is very well liked among my friends and anyone he meets. A gentle man with an uncompromising wit. He has carried on with the humor my grandfather had. He's a big guy standing six foot two and can be pretty intimidating, but actually he is a gentle giant. An example is when on a rainy day, there's a worm stuck on the sidewalk, he'll pick it up and put it back onto the grass. He loves animals well. When he was a little guy, he was always snuggling up to our cats. Later when he was on his own, he had Chip, his dog. Seeing them together, you'd think this dog was his actual son. Matt is now doing what he loves to do. Working with his hands and using his cleaver mind to solve problems, making a task more efficient building sets for the movies.

During my dancing, I met and befriended a young lady, who she referred to me as her best friend. That young lady was to become my sons wife and my daughter-in-law. They have two

Matthew and Ana

wonderful little girls, Emilia and Olivia. Emilia is into soccer and piano, making me so proud. She refers to herself as a scientist. Shen loves science. Olivia is in to everything. She's just a baby but with real potential. I'm putty in their hands. I love my little granddaughters.

Three years later, after Matthew was born, almost to the day, we conceived our daughter. The 4th of July was the date and nine months later Emily came out with a bang. Her name came about because of a restaurant Paula and I would go to for lunch every Friday. The place was called "Emily's". The name was, and is perfect, for our firecracker. Her middle name was taken from a song I've always loved that stole my heart. The song is "Clair." She was born on April 2nd. My cousin Donna was there at Emily's birth, and has always thought of Emily as someone very special to her. We brought Emily Clair home on Matthew's third birthday, she was also born at Huntington Memorial Hospital.

Both of our children were virtually free, because the doctor who delivered them both, also delivered Paula, and she worked for him during this time.

Back to our firecracker. Emily was born with a mind of her own, and no one could convince her otherwise. Even when she was in her two's and three's and took a fall or bumped her head, she didn't want consoling. She would go off by herself, fold her arms and sit in a corner until the hurt was over. What I loved about her the most, was her charm. She could get anything out of me. I couldn't resist.

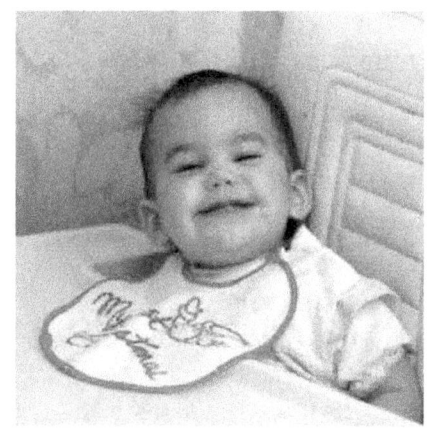

Emily Clair at one year

Emily became the daughter all dads dream of. She was full of life and full of energy. So many memories of her being both a challenge and a delight. I remember playing a little one on one basketball, she tickled me with her determination to get that ball in the hoop, She was so fast skirting around me like a sure footed gazelle. Her enthusiasm for performing charmed the whole family. It started with 'Dance and Twirl'. With no inhibitions she would perform for the family with so

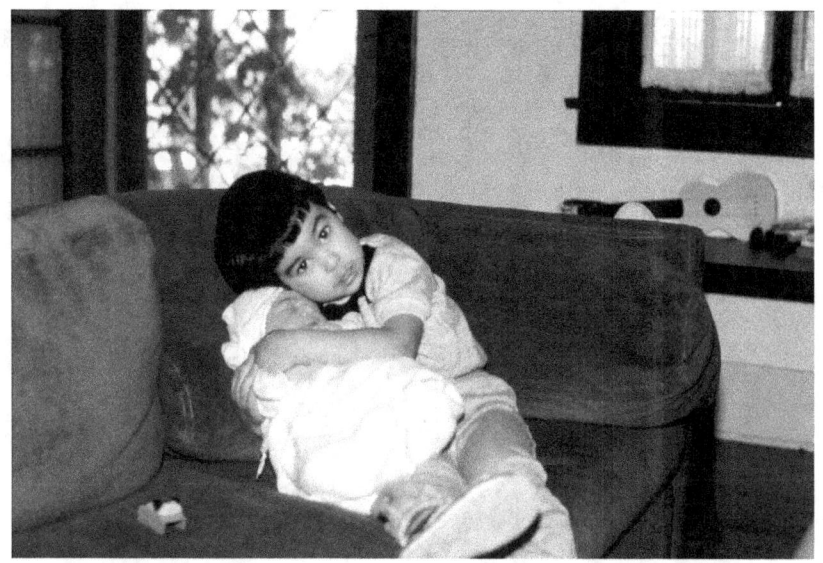
Matthew holding his new sister, on his third birthday

much confidence. She was a born performer. Then my little girl became a cheer leader while in middle school. Her squad cheered at Matts games, with very creative routines. They also competed against other schools and at the championship, her middle school squad actually beat Matts high school cheerleaders and won first place. It was pandemonium. My camera never stopped rolling.

Her next conquest was choir. In high school she became the soloist for the choir. She was flawless. I have to mention here, that when I was in my high school choir, we performed at the famous Shrine Auditorium in Los Angeles. But, my daughters choir did me one better. Her and her choir performed at the famed Carnegie Hall in New York. This was all in her first year in high school. At the same time while performing with the choir, she did an incredible performance for her church. She did a mime depicting the story of Christ. Again, I was right there capturing every moment of her very moving depiction. She and her choir would perform for retirement homes during Christmas.

Then, stardom struck my daughter, She went to the drama department of her high school and asked if she could audition for their

Snow play with the kids

next show. The drama teacher said, "But you're to even in drama, why do you want to do this?" Emily spoke up saying, "It looks like fun, can I try it please?" She was given a tape to watch and practice with and when she came back for the audition, she won hands down the lead in Cole Porter's "Anything Goes". I invited friends and family to se Emily's debut of singing, acting, and dancing. She was a natural. Her acting was flawless. So impressed by her, two of her teachers, they wound up paying for professional singing lessons. I remember her practicing with such enthusiasm. She was the lead once again for the next show, "Little Shop of Horrors". Wow! She knocked it out of the park. Her singing improved so much after those singing lessons.

Two more shows followed. "How to Succeed in Business without Really Trying", and she finished with her portrait of Dolly, in "Hello Dolly". By now, Emily had a following. People came from all over the Palm Springs area, where she lived, just to see Emily Crosthwaite, my daughter the performer. I know this because while seated in the auditorium, waiting for her performance of Hello Dolly, the people sitting next to me said they have been following Emily at all of her shows and were big fans. It was standing room only at all of her sold out shows. After each performance she was greeted a the stage door with screaming fans wanting her autograph. It was really something to witness. It was common knowledge that she would go pro, but when I asked her about it she said, "No Daddy, I was just having fun. It's too much work".

After high school, Emily married Dominic Balli. When their first two children, Selah and Solomon, came along, Emily took on the monumental task of homeschooling them. Again, she was a natural and a complete success. Her mother and I were so impressed at her tackling such a task, but she did it all in stride. Oh, and by the way, Paula and I were impressed with her amazing skill at parenting. I was blessed with their third child who came along six years after Solomon. Kingston came into this world with a spirit un for seen to any of us. Not homeschooled but taught by his mothcr, Emily, who became a teacher and taught her latest, in the classroom, with the same enthusiasm as her homeschooling. All three of Dominic and Emily's children excel in every aspect of life. Selah always had her head in a book and loved to write, not unlike her grandfather. She has heart of gold, spreading the word of her faith to the world. Solomon not only excelled in academics, but became their star quarterback in the high school flag football teem. It feels like Kingston has carried the gene I posses of dance. He's got the moves and talent that will serve him well as he is shaped into an adult. This one is also very bright, and I'm sure will make the world a better place.

Our lives continued year by year with memories and adventures as families do. Eleven years would pass before our little family came apart. Paula stayed in the house with the kids and I went to live with my cousin Donna. I'll never forget the look on my son's face when I walked out of the door. It tore at my heart but I had to leave. I came back every other weekend to do the chores I had always done. I'd clean the pool, do some yard work and any house maintenance needed. Up to this time Paula hadn't been working but

Emily and Dominic

she now took a job. Many times she would be working on weekends so I would be there with the kids while doing my chores.

I altered visits between my mother and my kids seeing Matt and Emily every other weekend. Sometimes I would bring them with me to visit their grandmother. During my time with my kids we would do things we didn't normally have time for when I was in the house. There was always something to be fixed or maintained. The yard, the pool, the house, a succession of never ending chores.

When I had the kids, it was playtime. I took them to museums, plays, out to dinner, the zoo, and air shows, to name a few. When Paula eventually sold the house and moved in with one of her sisters in Palm Springs, I would make the trip to the desert to visit the kids, especially when Emily had a performance or Matthew had a football game. Eventually, Paula would meet me halfway when I was to have them for the weekend if there was nothing special going on out there. Birthdays and holidays always brought us together as they still do to this day.

Emily married Dominic Balli and they have three children, Selah, Solomon and Kingston. My grandchildren. I'm so proud of them. They are all so special. Matthew has married as well and has brought two cherubs into this world, Emilia and Olivia, with his bride Ana, with whom I introduced him.

I was getting to the age where the on line dating was not working for me, so I did nothing for several months until I kicked myself off of the couch and headed over to the dance place Frankie asked me to find, and I've been there ever since. I'm there nearly every Saturday evening.

I've been attending the dances for over eleven years. The swing dance community is a special bunch of people. All very friendly and likable. Unlike a club, there's no alcohol and no fights. Just dance. At first I was intimidated by so many good dancers, but I faked it pretty well until I met Ruth. When we became an item she insisted we take lessons. In the following chapter I tell all about Ruth.

Matthew and Emily, my incredible children.

Before the Future
ALL ABOUT RUTH

I had just about given up when I realized my future was right in front of me. I had been seeing her every weekend for the last several months, so I took the plunge and asked her out. Previously disillusioned by the online dating services I'd tried, I came to do what I do best at meeting the ladies, dancing.

Ruth was one of the dance partners with whom I danced regularly. As a matter of fact, there were many to choose from, but most were much younger than me, and at age sixty-four I was ready to find my life partner, not find another fling. The first thing that attracted me to Ruth was the look on her face when she danced. That told me she was having the time of her life. I took that to mean that whatever she did, she would have that kind of enthusiasm. I was drawn to that look and couldn't get enough of it. Besides, she only five years my junior.

After a dance, I approached Ruth with a simple question, "What brought you to these dances?" She said her daughter told her to get out and find someone. After nine years of being single, she even suggested tennis. That didn't work, so dancing was the next trial for finding a mate. Ruth had been coming to the dance place where I met her for about a year. I had only been dancing there about six months. Her response to my question was, "I've been asked out by a few men, but I either wasn't ready or I was not interested." I told her something similar only through the online attempts I'd had. This is where I made my move. "Maybe we should go out?" I said. There wasn't much response until she said, "Why don't you give me your phone number and I'll give you a call?"

When I went back to the dance the next week, Ruth didn't show. I waited for that call all week, then the following week. It didn't come. I had given her my business card and wrote my home number on the back, but she called my office. The buzz around the office was, "Ron's got a girlfriend." At a sales meeting I was getting looks from the girls in the office. I returned Ruth's call filling her in on the "word" around the office and we got quite a chuckle.

We made arrangements to meet at a restaurant of Ruth's choice, "The Green Street Café" in Pasadena. I was there early, waiting for her. She walked up to my table. She looked so fresh and pretty. Her eyes sparkled with enthusiasm, and her smile put me at ease with its warmth. We began chatting. We first talked about the phone call to the office and laughed. She had a wonderful laugh. Jolly and almost out of control, which made me laugh all the more. We did a lot of laughing while getting to know each other. The evening was a complete success.

Our first real date was dinner and a movie. How original. I hadn't actually dated for quite a while, so a dinner and a movie seemed like the thing to do. We had Italian and saw whatever movie

210

was popular at the time. What we found out about each other that evening sealed it for me. We had so much in common, me being a designer and she being a photographer. What was most revealing for both of us is that we tend to mix up our words and sometimes-whole sentences. This created uncontrollable laughter that caused others to look at us as if wishing they were having as much fun as were.

At her front door, at the end of a perfect evening, we kissed. It was a good kiss. It was obvious there would be more passionate ones to come. As I bid her goodnight, Ruth said, "If you don't call me, I'll call you." On the way to my car my feet didn't touch the ground.

On our next date, I was given a tour of her townhouse and formal introductions to her two golden retrievers and two cats. The dogs, Buster and Jasmine, were happy and made friends with me easily. It took a while for the cats, Rambo and Oreo, to warm up to me. I was very pleasantly surprised at Ruth's taste in décor. Her home was sophisticated and tasteful with no fru-fru generally found in a woman's home. With my designer eye, I was very impressed. But, hold on! What I found in the garage made me a believer.

Ruth had recreantly closed her photography studio and, while in full operation, she would build her own sets and backdrops. In her garage was every tool a man would drool over, especially me. A man's woman. She even liked going to hardware stores. I was in heaven.

On some of our outings, we did just that. Getting lost in the aisles of Home Depot was more than a treat for me. We both liked discovering new things…just things. It was very cool. Of course, on occasion, we went because we actually needed something. Afterwards, we would treat ourselves to a cool yogurt or Starbucks coffee. I loved shopping with Ruth. Even at the market, we seemed to make it an adventure. That sharing of the simplest things is what I miss the most.

When our relationship became more serious, and the weekends spent together, is when our intimacy really took off. I would go the next day to her home, on Friday, after work, or the next day in the afternoon. Ruth confessed that she wasn't much of a cook, but why all the cookbooks? They were left over from her thirty-three year marriage where cooking was part of the "job." She raised three children who now have children of their own. Ruth did cook for me, though. Or rather prepared our first meal together, Peanut Butter and Jelly sandwiches. We laughed every time we remembered that special time. I took over in the kitchen, cooking some of my special dinners, finally having someone to share them with. She actually liked my cooking. While feeding Ruth, my ego was being fed. Each morning I would awake early and start the coffee maker we'd bought once we saw our relationship moving to the next level. Slowly Ruth would come down the stairs and sit on the sofa with one or both of her feline friends curling up on her lap while I prepared her coffee and served my sleepy girlfriend.

Right away, I would start talking. Ruth needed quiet time first thing in the morning, but I was prone to chatter away. Eventually, I got the message and tried my best to curb my morning mouth motoring. After our morning coffee, we would have our breakfast, then Ruth would hurry off to church while I made a few calls and waited for her to come home so we could start our day. In the early days, Ruth would stop off and get a doughnut and bring one for me. We'd decided together that maybe the doughnuts weren't the healthiest thing for us. However, after our big health decision, when she came back from church, there would be a tell-tale sign of white powder on her cheek or on her blouse. Catching her caused us to have our laugh for the day.

What I loved about Ruth was her vulnerability. She had a way of stumbling through life and laughing about it. I just enjoyed the heck out of her little faltering and loved her all the more for that. It made her so delightful to be around. She also had a third sense about her that I relied on time and time again. Her innate wisdom helped me more times than I can remember. In my writing and problem-solving

212

whether it was personal or dealing with family matters. I always took her advice seriously and was grateful for her input. We were at our best when we worked on projects together. Our two minds gave sensible solutions to any given challenge. She gave me credit for sticking to a task, and I was always amazed at her jumping right into a project and finishing it.

We got into a routine that worked well for a long time. Usually, we went to the dance place where we met and would enter separately. We decided to keep our relationship a secret. Each of us had formed friendships/dance partners through the many months, and we didn't want to interrupt that flow on the dance floor. It worked very well for both of us, except for the men who seemed interested in my Ruth. They didn't know that we would be together that night. It

Diamond Bar Rotary Club building one room homes for the less fortunate south of the border. Ruth and I are kneeled next to the proud recipient holding the key to his new home, his wife to his left.

was our little secret. I was even approached a couple of times by the ladies, but confessed that I had a girlfriend. It felt good saying those words. Being faithful made me even more attractive to my admirers.

The Music Center

"I don't need no stinking dance lessons" is what I would say whenever the subject came up. Eventually, I caved. Ruth and I took several lessons together, which made the dancing experience more enjoyable. We would practice in her living room and always end up with us laughing our heads off. Sometimes Ruth would get frustrated with me, because I didn't always follow the rules. "I dance to the music." I would say. But that didn't cut it. Even at the dances, she would get annoyed with me if I didn't do exactly what we had learned at the previous lesson. I guess my style of dancing wasn't exactly Ruth's cup of tea. I danced to the music and how it moved me. Ruth, on the other hand, wanted to dance according to the exact steps we had learned. Even after taking the lessons and me not conforming exactly, I did gain more confidence and started dancing with the more experienced dancers. Ruth said she had created a monster. I just kept on dancing.

Another activity that kept us busy was Ruth's Rotary Club. When I met her, she was in her first term as president of the Walnut Valley Rotary Club of Diamond Bar. Usually, only one term as president is the norm, but Ruth held a second term during our relationship. She stepped up to the plate when no one else would.

214

Cousin Donna, Aunt Dee Dee, Ruth and Me at Coronado Island

Everybody loved Ruth and how she kept everyone motivated. Although they laughed at her faux pas which made her all the more lovable, they responded with great respect for her organizational skills.

As president, Ruth shared many privileges with me. We traveled to conferences reserved only for incumbents, to Palm Springs three times and once in Arrowhead. Another additional trip organized by the club was when we went to the state capitol in Sacramento and got a VIP tour from senator Bob Huff. I became an honorary member of the Diamond Bar Rotary, doing volunteer work with Ruth. I had never experienced such giving of oneself as did Rotary club members. One of the most memorable things we did with Rotary was to go to Mexico and help build four small one room homes for poor people. We were one hundred strong and built four homes in one day. The homes were not much according to American standards, but they were palaces to the people who had been living in absolute squalor. When the key was handed to the young couple we built the home for it was quite moving.

What a great bunch of people I became acquainted with. All twenty-five or so members became my friends as we worked side by side doing volunteer work for various causes. I miss those friends. The parties, the trips and the many informal gatherings bonded us all, making me again so grateful to be a part of Ruth's world, which left me with a new set of friends.

Still another incredible thing Ruth shared with me was her season tickets to the Ahmanson Theater at the Music Center. I love the theater and had always wanted to go, but not alone. Now I had both the joy of attending the theater and someone very special to share them with.

On my sixty-fifth birthday, my very dearest friends decided to do something special. On our fiftieth, we all went on a cruise. Now, another milestone was upon us. I had been dating Ruth about five months, and it was now time for my special lady to meet my friends. I had told them about Ruth but they had never had the pleasure of meeting her until now. Our special birthday celebration was to take place in wine country, about 350 miles north, and was to be a three-day affair. We all drove up separately, and stopped mid-way to have lunch. They were introduced to Ruth. They immediately loved her. She was just being her incredible self. At breakfast in Napa, the next morning, Ruth asked my friends about me. Kathy said, "He's loyal, honest and, clean." That seemed to satisfy Ruth. We all had a fantastic time traveling to the various wineries while they got to know Ruth and she got to know my best friends. To this day, two of the wives of my old friends stay in touch with Ruth.

Ruth was very generous concerning my family. When I went to San Diego to visit my Aunt, who was wheelchair bound Ruth would accompany me. My aunt and Ruth immediately took a liking to each other. Aunt Dee Dee was at her best, keeping us all in stitches, coming up with off-the-wall humor which took Ruth by surprise. Each visit my cousin Donna, Ruth, and I would take my aunt out on the town, sometimes to the pier, sometimes to stroll along the wharf at Seaport Village, and sometimes to the local flea market. My aunt always looked forward to Ruth's visit. As time passed, my aunt became more demanding with regard to her care. Her daughter, Donna, could no longer be effective in her mother's care. A very difficult decision had to be made to sell Aunt Dee Dee's home and have her move into an assisted living home. Unfortunately, Ruth was there when our family was in this turmoil. We were in a bind with regards to funds to make the transition to enroll Aunt Dee Dee into a facility and the selling of her home. Ruth came up with the needed monies helping the family over the hump. She was incredible with her generosity. My family was stunned with gratitude. That was Ruth. She loved my aunt and just wanted to help. When the house eventually sold, many months later, Ruth was repaid and thanked for her caring assistance.

As the holidays neared, it was time to start a new tradition. Ruth's mother and father had always hosted a Christmas party in their home. Although they had passed the previous year, I convinced Ruth to continue the tradition. Ruth was the eldest of four sisters who all had families of their own, and they needed a place to go for the holidays. I told Ruth how my mother would have Christmas at her home for the family and how that tradition carried over to her twin, my Aunt Dee Dee, after my mother passed.

I helped decorate Ruth's home. She decided to have prime rib for the entree! I thought it a little much but she wanted this new tradition to be special for her first family holiday party. Together we made rum balls for the occasion, tasting them as we went along just to make sure they were just right. The rum had its effect on us, causing more uncontrollable laughter.

I met her family at this party. Much to her surprise, it was a big turnout. Family and neighbors attended and the party was a complete success. When Ruth's son met me, he immediately went to find his mother in the kitchen and asked, "Why didn't you just date Dad again?" Apparently, there was a striking resemblance between Ruth's ex and me. I didn't see it but her children sure saw it. I think it was the nose or something.

Ruth has two sons and one daughter. One of her sons lives in Texas and works as an army recruiter. While stationed in Germany, he met and married a local woman. They have a boy and a girl. Her other son lives locally in Chino Hills. He and his wife have two boys. Her daughter lives in Duarte and is married with three children, one boy and two girls.

Traditionally, Ruth celebrated her birthday with her local family by taking them out to dinner. Although we'd been dating only eight months, I felt it was appropriate to make an announcement. I told her family that I loved their mother very much and that we were happy to have found each other in this crazy world at our tender ages. There were congratulations all around. That was a huge thing for me to come right out and say. I'd never done anything like that before. I felt I owed it to her son and daughter to let them know my intentions and sincerity with their mother. I thought Ruth might have said something as a follow-up, but it didn't happen.

Another tradition Ruth had, regarding her birthday, was to have dinner at a special restaurant in Laguna Beach called, appropriately, The Beach House. I made reservations for an early dinner out on the patio so we could watch the sunset. Ruth had turned sixty that year, making it very special for both of us. We watched the sun slowly disappear over the horizon of the Pacific while we held hands. After a delicious meal and a glass of wine, we took a walk along the beach arm in arm. It was another magical night for both of us. We didn't want the evening to end, so we went to the local theater and saw a movie. We got home very late, but there was still time for intimacy. The next day, I called the restaurant and made standing reservations for the next hundred years.

We had one more of those special birthdays at the Beach House, but it was to be our last. Our relationship began to become strained. My son had moved back, into my home for the third time and I'm afraid I took out my frustrations on Ruth. I didn't even realize what I was doing until it was too late. Ruth said that ever since my son moved back I had changed. She said I wasn't the man she'd fallen

218

in love with. I had no answer to this shocking news. I hadn't been aware of how I had affected our relationship. I was totally blindsided. I tried telling Ruth that I was still the same person, but it was too late for her. She had been sensing this for a while and hadn't said anything until she was completely sure. It was over. I was once again alone. She made plans to move to Oregon and I was again in shock. I said "I will move to Oregon with you." She reminded me that at one time I had said that I didn't want to leave my family and friends. I tried to back peddle, saying, "That was then, and now. I will move with you." Again it was too late. She was set on her new path. She said she discovered that she actually liked living alone.

Not until years later was I told by my two friends, Kathy and Andrea who kept in touch with Ruth, what reason she gave them for wanting out of the relationship. They said she told them that I was not letting her make her own mind up about things. It's still not clear to me exactly what I did wrong. I only wish Ruth had told me how I was putting distance between us, and let me know how to make it right. I'm thinking maybe there just wasn't enough love on her part to make that effort. Whatever it was, I, through my actions, lost my chance of a loving partnership...a regret that will always haunt me.

Ruth had moved to Grants Pass, Oregon, much to my dismay. She'd put miles between us and has moved on not needing me in her life any longer. For a while, we kept in touch through email and an occasional phone call. She says she's very happy, and I'm happy for her, but I can't help wishing things were different. Ruth got married three years after her move, and both Andrea and Kathy met her husband. They say he is a very nice man. Ruth is happy with him. That's all that matters.

Poem written about Ruth on the following page

I ONCE HAD A GIRLFRIEND

I've had my share of relationships
I've been married with children
I have many good friends
Then I met someone who for once, I felt I belonged to
We met doing what I love doing, dancing
She was cautious at first
I was ready to commit
We connected beyond my expectations
We had more in common than any other
Our lives became wonderfully filled
So many things to do
So much fun doing them
I had a girlfriend
All of my friends loved her
I was happy
We spent time with friends and family
We spent time with each other
I had a girlfriend
I was no longer alone
I was happy

Then it was over
We parted friends
But I can't forget what we've shared
I can't forget sharing our first cup of coffee of the day
I can't forget taking our walks
I can't forget our solitary moments
I can't forget working together
I can't forget laughing together
I can't feel that happiness I found
I'm alone again
I once had a girlfriend

RENEWED INNOCENCE
A second chance

I admit, I could sometimes be called a dance snob. When one becomes proficient at something, we tends to want to keep up with our challenge to move forward. As in skiing, tennis, or even dance. However, as a single man with eyes that wandered. I noticed a new young lady who just came onto the scene. I also observed she was definitely a beginner. So being the dance snob that I am, I chose not to ask her to dance. One evening, they called for all the birthday dancers to come onto the floor for their birthday dance, and there she was. Well, we are asked to gather around the birthday person and give them their birthday greeting dance. So, I cut in and gave my usual celebratory dance, but once I caught her glance, I was stunned by her incredible smile. I'm a sucker for a great smile.

There I was, asking this young lady to dance, from time to time. As we got to talking and getting to know each other, I mentioned the two books I had written. Her response was, "I've never met an author, I have so many questions". I asked for her phone number, saying that I would be glad to answer any questions she had. That was the start of it. It was December 31st, 201,7, at 8 pm when I made the call. We talked right up to when the ball dropped, bringing in the new year. Four hours straight. I had never talked that long to anyone on the phone. I'm always on the lookout for a pretty face.

The next time we met on the dance floor, it was all smiles on both sides. When it was time to go home, I walked her to her car. I took her in my arms and pulled her close, giving her a soft kiss. As she opened her eyes, she leaned in for another, then suddenly a car passed by and she immediately tried to hide. We saw it as awkward to be smooching where we could be seen by other dancers. But that didn't stop us. From then on, we found ourselves wanting more of this forbidden pleasure. It was decided that she follow me to my home, where we could continue uninterrupted. That became our pattern week after week. Our routine was, once we arrived at my home, to throw the sofa pillows onto the floor, making room for us to lie down next to each other so we could cuddle...It was a fantasy come to life, making out like high school kids in the back seat of a car. Never in my wildest dreams could I imagine this could ever happen at my advanced age of seventy-seven. But there we were, throwing all caution to the wind. What made it so much more unexpected was that Lisa was 24 years

Lisa and her daughter Laura

younger than me. She knew our age difference after having read my books, one of which was where I mentioned my age. When I confronted her about our age difference, she was okay with it and said that it didn't matter.

Our time was limited to no more than an hour. It turns out that Lisa had a special needs daughter who couldn't be left alone for very long. Once she was put to bed at 8 o'clock sharp, she was okay for a while, but Lisa had to be home to be there for her daughter in case she woke up. The girl was 15 years old with the mind of a 4-year-old. That's why that first call wasn't until 8 p.m., and that is also why our cuddling could not last into the night. Lisa also had two teenage boys. Her divorce had very recently been finalized, and it was what led her to reach out for a fresh start by way of social dancing. She carried on her marriage for those many years, but a divorce was long overdue. Her ex was a beer-drinking sports fan... sitting in front of the

TV, beer in hand, was his m.o. He took little interest in raising his children, especially his daughter. It was all Lisa. I came in on a white horse, rescuing her from a life of mental cruelty. Lisa had never been given flowers. I showered her with bouquets. She had never had anyone open a door for her. I opened doors for her at every opportunity. I'm treating Lisa like a lady. She had almost forgotten what it was like to have any respect in her life.

As our relationship developed, we started exploring this new thing called boyfriend/girlfriend. One of her sons was a budding artist. I agreed to show him around at my alma mater, Art Center. He was dueling impressed by this prestigious art college. After our meeting, he went his way, and Lisa and I went to the nearby Desconso Gardens, a tranquil oasis in the city that was open to the public. As we strolled along one of the paths, I pulled Lisa off the path behind a bush and swept her into my arms with a loving kiss. Romance was in the air, and I took full advantage. We started going places, I would have never gone on my own. I loved having someone by my side to share doing things out of my comfort zone. I introduced Lisa to her first opera. We went to clubs and plays. It turned out that we both, in our past, played golf, so every Saturday for quite a while, we would play golf in the morning, then go out for lunch, then go dancing that night. But the most intimate times of all were when I would have her over for dinner. I went all out and bought candles, dessert bowls, and wine glasses. I had never, in my whole life, done anything like this. I lit candles, created a playlist of romantic music, and prepared meals with a theme. Chinese, Mexican, Italian, and even Russian themes. I wined and dined my lady with all the trimmings. Holding hands across the table with the soft candle glow, we sipped our wine, peering into each other's eyes. These meals went on for months, and from time to time, Lisa invited me to her home for dinner.

When I first met her daughter, knowing her condition, I took care to be extra sensitive as I spoke to her. Laura would sit in her chair surrounded by coloring books and crayons. She also played with matchbook cars. She even had a play station garage where she would drive the cars up a ramp and pretend to put gas in her cars and drive off with a zoom. Laura constantly watched cartoons on her television. That's all she watched: cartoons. Eventually, I introduced her to Laurel and Hardy, which she loved. We got along pretty well. Of course, there was very little said. She had no social skills whatsoever. Lisa was impressed that I got along with her daughter so well. She said no other adult took the time to try to communicate with her.

Meeting her sons was an altogether challenging experience. The older son was, in my observation, odd. He spoke very fast, almost to the point where it was difficult to understand him. He was the artist, so I tried my best to speak of what we had in common. The younger son was extremely shy and reserved. He was very bright and didn't smile much. He would look away as he spoke. There wasn't much we could talk about, but I sensed he trusted me, at least. He got along with his sister, whereas his brother didn't want anything to do with he

When Lisa and I reappeared at the dances, we tried to keep our relationship a secret. But eventually, it got out. Everyone knew Lisa was quite a bit younger than me, and some of the guys teased me about it. "You dog you". Our lives went on for the rest of that year, but tensions began to rear their ugly head. There were times when Lisa didn't always listen to me as I was speaking to her. Or, it seemed that way. When I confronted her about this, she vehemently denied my accusation. This happened more than once. She just had this habit of not showing any response as I spoke to her. It frustrated me to the point where I kept up my inquisitions. The friction grew.

There was a time when they gave away free red potatoes at the dance, and I thought it was a given to take them home for the upcoming Thanksgiving dinner. But Lisa said no, she wanted to buy her own potatoes. I should have left it alone, but I persisted. That led to even more hostilities. Then the coup de grâce was when I said, Why are you so sensitive?'. Wrong! I kept, unknowingly, driving a wedge between us. The next day, we had our Thanksgiving dinner, but that was to be our last gathering. She called and said it was time to break it off. We agreed to meet at a restaurant near my home to exchange our possessions. I had given her a painting I did while in college. It was an original painting that I thought would have meant a lot to her. She didn't even want to keep it. All things said, it came down to she wanted to grow old with someone closer to her age. We both knew our relationship couldn't last forever. The age difference was too great, and the inevitable was on the table. I just wasn't ready for it to end so soon. In a little under 14 months, my fantasy world crumbled around me.

DOWN BUT NOT OUT
Until my time is up

Well, it finally happened. My body started to give up, showing me my life could end at any moment. My daughter, Emily, and granddaughter, Selah, visited me during my short stay at Huntington Hospital, where both my children were brought into this world.

"But you eat well and dance. This shouldn't happen to you." And then it did. As a result, I now have two stents keeping my blood flowing to and from my heart. First time in my 84 years I've begun to take meds for the first time. It wasn't a heart attack but a warning. Besides the meds, I'm now taking vitamins by the tons. Oh well, it beats the alternative. My doctors said to keep dancing and keep doing what I'm doing, regarding my eating habits. I do and I will. It hasn't stopped me from dancing. As a matter of fact, I now dance as much as I ever have, keeping up with many much younger than me.

My stamina has wavered a bit, so I pace myself. Just after the hospital, I started a physical therapy course to strengthen my heart and lungs. After 28 weeks, I was ready to get out of that torture chamber. I then started my doing my walks a couple of times a week.

Nancy Mead and me
Lasting Friendships

Nothing much more to say regarding my physical health, but I seem to slip back in time too often. For a time there, I thought I should see a therapist, but that didn't work out. I'm pretty much okay except for a few daily slumps. I get out of that 'down' by the end of the week, when it's dance time. I enjoying the company of others and moving my feet to the rhythm of the music. During the week, my time is generally spent writing and giving myself a time-out to watch any one of my 70 movies I've collected on a playlist. I feel I'm a pretty good judge of movies. When searching for new movies I haven't seen on T V, I'll give it a test of a few minutes. If a movie falls short in any one of the categories, like dialogue, storyline, or authenticity, I'll move on.

228

I have a few favorites, of course. "As good as it gets" with Diane Keaton and Jack Nicholson somehow lets me see myself in the scenario of finding love at an older age. "Definitely Maybe" is another movie that lets me move in my mind to a fantasy of an involvement with each of the three women featured in the movie. Not many have even heard of the movie, but it's one of my favorites. There are a few action-type films in there as well, like "Raiders of the Lost Ark", "Star Wars", but one of my all-time favorites is "Ben Hur". It holds up better than any of the films of that genre. These are just a few of my 70 selections. I won't bore you with the rest. But they certainly do not bore me!

Thank goodness for my time with my son and his family. About once a week, I'm invited to dinner. On the menu is Salmon. Every time I'm there for dinner, it's Salmon. That's when I get my Omega-3 for the week. I love watching my two little granddaughters grow. With each visit, there's something new. My weekly attendance at Emilia's soccer games gets me out of the house on a Saturday afternoon to catch some sun and cheer on the team. I always reminded my son of his soccer games when he was a kid. From his soccer games to his football games, I was always there. Emily was in Dance and Cheer, and her shows were always so entertaining. She had all the moves down and eventually took her talents to the cheerleading squad in both middle school and high school. Then, of course, she had her very successful performances on the stage.

To my regret, I don't see my daughter and her children as much as I would like. Emily has a busy schedule with raising three children, being a pastor's wife, and teaching school. I try to check in once in a while, but it's never enough. Our get-togethers at Christmas and some birthdays are about all I get a chance to be with them. I've never been able to be a part of those grandchildren as much as I wish. But as they've grown, I couldn't be prouder. All three are exceptional. Selah is the sweetest, with a charm that warms anyone lucky enough to get to know her. Solomon has grown into a formidable guitarist and quarterback for his flag football team in high school. And then there's Kingston. The youngest of the three certainly holds his own. Very accomplished in his academics. He excels in math and, overall, like his big brother and sister, is extremely bright. My daughter and her husband, Dominic, have done an exceptional job nurturing their children to be, I'm sure, extraordinary adults. I feel so lucky to have five wonderful grandchildren. You never know how kids turn out when they first appear, but then, wow, I never would have guessed I would be a grandfather to such incredible children.

Funny how, as the years pass, they bring back memories of innocence. I just can't get through the day without letting the past give me comfort. It goes by so fast, but only at the time you're reflecting. While it's happening, time stands still. Time is the most valuable of all. I find myself wasting time when I shouldn't, but I guess that could be called downtime. Giving myself a time-out just to do nothing. Then I say to myself, there's only so much time left, so make the most of it. I have to say, I've given my life a once-over and I find that I have done quite a bit with my time. Sure, I have regrets, but who doesn't? I'm a victim of my environment, even though I will admit I've made some wrong decisions. I live with those wrong decisions daily, whether good or bad. When looking back at what I believe, it led me to turning right or left or avoiding or plowing through, I know I've affected others, sometimes for the better, and to my dismay, disappointed others greatly. I will not make excuses for my behavior because it wouldn't do any good. I know that. I'm only grateful for having lived as long as I have and for having had the friendships and experiences I've enjoyed. I'll take it all with me when my time is up. I only hope I might be remembered for any good I shared while I was here.

Our yearly Christmas Nerf Battle at Emily's home

\\

Before the Future
MY BUDDIES

George   Pat   Bill   Mark   Ron

We were known as The Five Families, a term Bill coined from the Godfather movie series. The Hardys, The Morans, The Smaws, The Jason's and The Crosthwaite's. I was best man at Bill, George, and Pat's weddings and a Huppah Holder at Mark's wedding, and I held his son Willie at his Bris. Bill was my best man at my wedding, and Pat and George were groomsmen at my wedding, along with my cousin Rick. I had to choose family over Mark. Had there been more bridesmaids, Mark would have been included, but I had to include my cousin Rick.

Pat Moran, George Hardy, and I were all born in late November on the 26th, 28, and 29th, respectively. When we turned twenty one we three celebrated that momentous year and have been celebrating ever since. Eventually, I added Bill to our group and then Mark. Along with their girlfriends, then, their wives, our celebrations grew into fun and memorable get-togethers year after year without fail. On our fiftieth, we went on a cruise down to Baja. On our sixtieth, we celebrated on the Queen Mary. On our sixty-fifth, we went to wine country for three days. On our seventieth, we spent three days and two nights in LaGuna Beach. On our seventy-fifth, we spent four days in Solvang.

Another tradition that soon followed was our annual baseball picnics. Each year, we would gather at South Pasadena park with family and friends. We would bring food to share, and each year, there would be another addition to our gathering. Sometimes it would be new friends or family members, but the most welcome was when, after each of our marriages, we started bringing our children one by one. Many of my students also attended.

Everyone played baseball. Young and old. We would also set up a net and play volleyball. Sometimes we would choose up teams and have a tug-of-war.

On other occasions, we would have a beach party at Huntington Beach. We'd stay till the sun went down and would gather around the fire pit, roasting marshmallows and hot dogs. Mark would break out his guitar, and we would all sing our hearts out on those warm summer evenings. Sometimes we all ventured down to San Diego Bay. My aunt had a power boat, and we would attempt water skiing. Other times, cousin Rick brought his Jet Skis for us to ride. When it was my daughter's turn to ride, I was on the back holding on for dear life. Emily drove that jet ski like a madwoman, and she was only ten. What fun! The most memorable time was when my son Matt, Mark, Pat, and I went out into the bay on a small rowboat. We were about twenty feet from shore when Mark started rocking the boat. Back and forth, back and forth, till it toppled over and dumped us all into the waist-deep water. We all waded to shore, soaking wet, and laughing our heads off. We played horseshoes, threw a football around, and generally had the time of our lives. At the time, my

234

mother was wheelchair bound but that didn't stop her from having a great time as well.

Mark and Roz had a cabin at Lake Arrowhead and shared it with all of us. Sometimes it was husbands and wives, and sometimes it was just the boys. They had a boat we would take out on the lake. One time I took my kids up there, and Mark's son, Willie, Matt, and Emily had a blast diving off the pier and enjoying speeding over the lake in the boat.

One of the most memorable times up there in the mountains was with the boys when all five of us went up for a long weekend. We cruised the lake and walked around in the village, taking in the sights. Food time we all shared our expertise. One evening, Mark prepared a steak dinner, and another night Pat shared his special salmon dish. I enjoyed supplying the breakfasts. That last night around the dinner table as the wine flowed, Mark and Bill got into a rousing conversation that kept us all in stitches for hours. Pat told his infamous joke, "Do you snuff Birds ?" He tried his best to get it out, but kept stumbling over and over with the words. I videotaped the whole thing all the while trying to hold the camera steady. I've never laughed so hard. It just kept getting funnier and funnier as the evening wore on.

Another tradition that lasted many years until age and immobility caught up to some was our annual golf game. Bill was the best golfer among us and took the game very seriously. I was next best but was just playing to be with my friends. George was probably the least athletic, but was determined to hit that little white ball the best he could. Pat wanted to kill that poor little ball. He would grind his teeth and swing as hard as he could, trying to slam that ball as far as he could. His ball usually landed off to the left into the trees. We would spend way too much time looking for his ball. Mark was funny. He would call his club a bat and always swing as though he were playing baseball. Another thing Mark would do was to tease Bill relentlessly. Just as serious Bill would go to swing his club, and Mark would blow a whistle. Another time when Bill looked away, Mark put an exploding golf ball on the tee. It was made of chalk, and when hit, it seemed as though it exploded. Mark always wanted to wager on who would win, but we agreed that whoever got the lowest score, the others would have to pay for lunch. Bill had a lot of free meals. But... the time when we laughed the most was when poor Bill accidentally dropped his brand new canvas golf bag into the lake. Then he proceeded to play through, hitting a tree. A second time, after hitting the tree, he swung again and hit the same tree again. We were on the ground laughing. I happened to video most of that as well. Another laugh that is hard to repeat. Thank goodness Bill could laugh about it later.

We've all had our good and bad times. Struggles and successes. But through it all, we've remained loyal friends. These friends will always come first, no matter what. They are like brothers. They are family. They are my buddies.

To this date, we've lost Bill, Pat, and Mark. George and I are the only ones left. Mark and George lost their wives, Roz and Linda respectively. I got divorced, so out of the ten, we are down to four. Pat's wife Andrea, Bill's wife Kathy, George, and me. We never got to bring in our 80's together.

The Five Families at one of our yearly birthday dinners

AFTERWORD

My stories of family, friends, and lost loves have kept me traveling through the years. Those years, are the sum of me, and of the loves that are gone forever. I now live in a reality world, where I treasure these memories. I can only, from this time on, move forward one day at a time.

I don't expect love again. I only have thoughts of what it would be like to have any of them survive to this day.

I look forward to any time I'm with my children and my grandchildren. Very few of my family are left. I am now the elder in my immediate family, which seems strange but it's a fact...I'm the "old guy."

Standing at the doorway of life, I knock. I wait for the door to open to see how it will all end.

Final thoughts:

Reflect the good times in your daily life and learn from your mistakes, not repeating them if at all possible. Keep the child within to draw on the innocence when it's appropriate. Love the moment and do not regret the things over which you had no control. Be aware, be prepared, and stay positive. Be there for loved ones in their time of need and accept their help when it's needed. Being too proud won't win you any medals. Finally, when the time comes, be thankful for all that was good in your life and go out with a smile.

NOTES